Granitaria

Granitaria

*From the Files of FBI Agent
Allison "Alli" Chapman*

a novel by

Marco Savage

Copyright © 2018 by Marco Savage.

Library of Congress Control Number: 2018913684
ISBN: Hardcover   978-1-9845-6677-5
              Softcover   978-1-9845-6676-8
              eBook   978-1-9845-6675-1

All rights reserved. No part of this book may be reproduced or transmitted in any form or by any means, electronic or mechanical, including photocopying, recording, or by any information storage and retrieval system, without permission in writing from the copyright owner.

This is a work of fiction. All of the characters, names, incidents, organizations, and dialogue in this novel are either the products of the author's imagination or are used fictitiously.

Any people depicted in stock imagery provided by Getty Images are models, and such images are being used for illustrative purposes only.
Certain stock imagery © Getty Images.

Print information available on the last page.

Rev. date: 11/15/2018

To order additional copies of this book, contact:
Xlibris
1-888-795-4274
www.Xlibris.com
Orders@Xlibris.com
778062

Recently I happened to catch a news program. The anchor was interviewing an author about his new book. He asked a question I'd heard many times before. But it never really took hold until I was writing my first book. The anchor asked,

"What was your inspiration to write this novel?" The answer the author gave, was also something I've heard many times.

"Well, I had a dream. When I woke up, I began to write."

I have no idea how many accomplished writers have said those words, but in my case it's true.

Many years ago, I had a dream. But it was not exactly about this location. Though similar, it had a different reason for being.

Granitaria is a place. It is home to a very special people. People that never left the cave. When most of us walked out, a small number continued inward. Searching for safety and protection for their families.

Granitaria is also the story of a Phoenix FBI agent. She is given the task of investigating three identical murders. She eventually partners with a Phoenix police detective. Soon, the duo become keepers of a great secret. One that could change the history of the world.

Granitaria- from the files of FBI agent Allison "Alli" Chapman, has many sides. But mostly it's a fun fantasy. I'm also working on the sequel. -White Candle- from the files of FBI agent Allison "Alli" Chapman. Hopefully Alli will have many adventures. Many stories to tell.

Definitions of the word

GRANITARIA

1. A type of moth (Lobocleta Granitaria)

2. A type of building material

3. A place

Jacket

"Alli, are you alright?" Tim instinctively stepped in front of the FBI agent, shielding her from the attack.

"Go get him, damn it! I'll be fine." She wasn't. She was scared. Her body was not responding. Her back hurt where she landed. Cave floors are hard.

Alli Chapman wanted to get up and run, but she was confused. Her eyes blurred and her muscles were tight. Where was she? What was that smell? It was familiar. Like cookies! She could smell cookies like when she was young. And gravy. The white milk gravy her Grandmother made from fried chicken! What was going on? She felt a little sick.

Then Alli was back. Back in the cave. Her ears rang and the back of her head hurt. That was from the fall.

What seemed like several minutes, took a single moment. Tim was right there protecting her. He never left her side.

"Go on Tim, I'm Ok." For Alli, embarrassment was the worst emotion. "Get off your ass and fire your weapon!" She said under her breath. Cutter and her partner were down the cavern, out of sight. Tim was chasing the bad guy and she was lying around. Alli was furious!

Alli Chapman had just witnessed Cutters abilities for the first time. The vision of him floating was permanently etched in her head. A human being floating in mid air without any apparent means of doing so, can have a huge impact on even the most well trained FBI agent.

She yelled down the cavern at whomever would listen. "If we don't have this technology, we've got to get it!" However that didn't seem likely. They would have to steal it and that she would never do.

In the months to come, FBI agent Chapman would think about floating people every time she entered a confined space. Was she being obsessive? Maybe not. Maybe she was reminding herself to run from evil. Like a trigger for preservation. Left overs from when man walked out of the cave. Simple survival.

After all, what more do we really need than shelter, food, and fire.

"Alli, are you all right?" Tim instinctively stepped in front of the FBI agent. Shielding her from the attack.

"Go get him damn it! I'll be fine." She wasn't. Alli was scared. Her entire body was slow to respond. Her back hurt where she landed. Cave floors are hard.

Alli Chapman wanted to get up and run. But she was confused. Her eyes blurred and tight muscles were very painful. Where was she? She couldn't focus. And what was that smell? It was familiar. Like cookies. She could smell cookies like when she was young. And gravy. The white milk gravy her Grandmother made from fried chicken. What was going on? She felt a little sick.

Then Alli was back. Back in the cave. Her ears rang and the back of her head hurt. That was from the fall.

What seemed like several minutes took but a single moment. Tim was right there. Protecting her. He never left her side.

"Go on Tim. I'm ok." Embarrassment was the worst emotion. As her partner rose and started down the cavern in pursuit, she pushed herself up.

"Get off your ass and fire your weapon!" Alli was furious. Her partner was chasing the bad guy down the tunnel and she was just lying around.

Rising from the depths of the Atlantic Ocean, a bright disc slowly ascends. Water cascades from the dome of the craft, spilling off the sides. Back lit by white light as it falls. The craft fits the precise description Christopher Columbus made in his journal in 1492. Then he claimed to have seen an object rise from the ocean, hover, then disappear into the night sky. Although he never saw it again, the story was retold by Columbus and his men when they returned to Spain.

Now, hundreds of years later, the scene is repeated. A shiny ship comes and goes. Always at the same longitude and latitude. Taking advantage of the Earth's curvature to hide. Though human technology has improved with the invention of satellites, these discs are not concerned with detection. They know that if sighted their presence is ignored. The usual reaction of governments on every continent. Always worried about their grip on man kind. Admitting the existence of extraterrestrials would certainly unsettle world populations. Proving politicians were never in control.

The beings in control of this advanced technology, are not going far. A near by planet in our solar system has caught their attention, and warranted the trip. However, they would return soon. It was very important to keep an eye on Earth at such a crucial time.

Chapter 1

"Roger Bower ranch, on approach. ETA, two minutes." A helicopter makes contact with the landing pad at a private ranch in Texas. The owner built a radar out building on the edge of his property so multiple chopper flights could be monitored. It was primarily used for special occasions. This was a special day. It was tailgate time in Texas!

Summer turns to fall and kids head back to school, but nothing gets them through winter like football.

Together with the football season is another, albeit more recent tradition. Pre-game tailgating!

Americans love football. Women love it. Men dream the season never ends.

Each state has their own football traditions, and Texas is well known for its football flavor. In Austin, being a Long Horn fan is religious. They should have churches just for football. What substitutes are large tailgating parties. The Bower family tailgate is one of the largest. Every year a few hundred local residents descend on the Bower property. It's bluejeans, Bar-BQ and beer. Good times, Texas style!

In the middle of a clover meadow, a large area gets soaked with water and four wheel drive pick ups whip it into a muddy track. In front of a stand of Junipers, a stage is erected for bands to play on. This draws the Austin party crowd out in large numbers.

Year after year, game after game it is always a great time!

The party kicks off in the morning and runs into the night, but come game time, those that have tickets head back to the stadium. Others watch big screens, or listen to the radio.

The owners daughter, Kate Lynn Bower, plays the part of hostess. She liked to get on the microphone to welcome guest and lead everyone in a short prayer. She introduced the bands, helped serve food and generally was the face of the Bower family.

Kate Lynn along with her boyfriend Buddy, made sure everyone got home safe. Rides were provided for anyone who drank too much at the trough. Literally, there was a trough!

The festivities finished up between nine and ten. The bands and caterers packed up by mid-night. With their duties complete, Kate and Buddy drove his pick-up down to the mud pit. The Moon was hanging low over the Texas hill country. Kate Lynn thought it was romantic. There was a couple in another truck, but they were making out and would soon be gone.

Kate scooted across the seat and whispered in her boyfriends ear. "Bet you didn't see a pair of jeans like mine tonight." Buddy didn't answer. Instead he was looking out of his side window. Something caught his eye. A bright light way off above the trees. Just as he was going to point it out to Kate Lynn, she announced that someone was walking out of the Junipers.

"Look Buddy, they're all wearing overalls. Are they working around here?"

"I don't know. I've never seen them before. Seems kinda late." They watched the men cross the meadow and out of sight. At the same moment Buddy received a big kiss from his gal. Their agenda was set for the evening.

Several hours later Kate woke up. She was all alone in the truck and began calling for her boyfriend.

"Buddy, Buddy, what's going on?" She stumbled out of the truck and there on the ground was her boyfriend. Next to him were the kids from the other pick up. They were lying face down with their heads turned all the way around. Each one had their arms straight out to the side. Kate began screaming! The Texas teen could not look away from the horror that was once her boyfriend. His eyes were wide. His neck snapped and his head spun around. Her eyes darted from body to body. They all looked the same as Buddy. She began yelling, NO! She repeated it over and over as she started to run. Kate ran until she collapsed near a dirt road that ran through the ranch. "No, No! Poor Buddy."

The authorities were already out looking for the kids. Kate Lynn's parents had alerted them. It was way to late in the evening. The young couple should have been home. They found Kate first. She was scraped up on her arms and legs, but otherwise unharmed.

"Buddy is dead." She was so quiet, the Travis County Police could hardly make out what she was saying. One officer bent down, "What did you say honey?" The question made her angry. "He's dead! My Buddy is dead!" With that she began crying and repeating, "No!" Just part of her shock they guessed. She repeated it every few minutes then suddenly she stopped and looked straight into the eyes of an officer. "There were men. Men in overalls. Walked right in front of our truck!" Then Kate Lynn Bower collapsed on the ground.

When the authorities discovered the murdered kids, several officers got sick. Men with years of experience searched the trunks of police vehicles for surgical masks. If for no other reason than to cover their revulsion. They had never seen anything like this.

The police tried to question Kate Lynn, but no one believed she had done the crime. This was a large man or more than one like the girl said. For the Travis County cops this was a cold case before it got started. Kate was the only apparent witness and she had passed out in the truck. There were hundreds of folks at the party so someone had to have seen something, but when question the family said it was open to whomever wanted to come. No invitations were sent out. They did not know everyone. A bulletin was put out asking for information on workman or utility employees in the area. None were found. Everyone was just grateful that Kate Lynn survived. Even if she would never be the same.

The truth was, there were men in the meadow and they wore overalls. Kate Lynn had told the truth. However, they had nothing to do with the murders. If Buddy had just looked at the trees and not the light in the sky, he would have seen the real killer. The man that would take his life that night. Someone he may have recognized. The killer was at the tailgate. He drank right along side other loyal Texans. He waited for everyone to leave so he could use his special ability.

His gift had many layers. One of which the ability to defy gravity. Though limited, it allowed the killer to float short distances. In this case, up into the trees. To watch and wait. Wait for the men in overalls to leave. He had to hide from them. He killed in private. He killed at a distance.

When he finished, he gently floated down from a large branch, and strolled through the meadow. Toward the mud pit. The lone survivor had long since run off screaming something he could not understand. The terror she was experiencing was obvious. He loved it. It made him feel content. In control.

He wanted to survey his kill. The police would not be there for some time. He felt completely comfortable. When he reached the two vehicles parked by the mud pit, he stood over the three bodies. Curious how they looked. Like some form of art. He thought himself an artist. A purveyor of a new world. In truth, he was a monster. He enjoyed his time in Texas. It was his first stop. His first step toward his new world. As he walked away, he said to himself,

"Ya all come back now!" There was no doubt that he would.

Chapter 2

The southwest part of the United States has always had a reputation for supernatural events. Like the UFO crash in Roswell, New Mexico or the Hopi Indians stories of strange lights in the mountains around their reservation. It is part of their folklore and tribal history to associate themselves with visitors from other worlds. Many Indian cultures kept track of "Star People." Five thousand year old rock paintings show what look like beings in space suits adorned with round helmets. Very similar to what our astronauts look like today.

Modern day Arizona has it's own UFO story. The now infamous "Phoenix Lights!" In the mid 1990's, a bank of lights moved across the sky over Phoenix. It was seen by thousands. Even the Governor of the state followed them across town. Though at first he did not admit it, he would eventually affirm that the lights were not of Earthly origin. It was definitely a craft. Unlike anything he had ever seen. Triangular in shape with lights along the under side, and very large. This caused him a certain amount of political grief, but he stuck to his story and promised to continue his investigation. In the days and weeks that followed, many came forward with similar descriptions of the craft. On that particular evening, there were actually two full sets of lights. The ones mounted under the craft that traveled for several miles across the valley and some that came later. Very similar, but stationary against the night sky. Then one by one they went out, without moving too far from where they were first seen. Many believed the second set of lights were an attempt to cover-up for the first. Whatever the case, the sighting was incredible and remains a highly debated event in UFO circles.

FBI agent Allison "Alli" Chapman loved the Phoenix Lights stories. She had not seen them herself, but was fascinated that it took place in her home town. It was thrilling when a call came in reporting some strange apparition, or bumps in the attic. It was a real kick when a UFO report crossed her desk. By mistake, of course. It should have been delivered elsewhere. But she liked to announce such a report to her fellow agents by declaring,

"We're being invaded again!" And hold the file up for all to see.

This action succeeded in getting huge laughs around the office. However, if a report like that did come in, it was immediately turned over to a Special Department of the bureau. Never to be heard from again. The same agents that laughed at such reports, secretly questioned their importance. And their validity. Why did anyone care? Why have a Special Department at all.

Alli was two hours away from a four day weekend when the call came in from the Phoenix police. It sounded horrible. Three dead in different parts of the valley. She could hear the stress in the detectives' voice. Alli knew some of these guys and could tell when the scene was out of the ordinary. She was asked to meet at the first victims residence. The Phoenix cops felt the FBI should see the crime scenes before the bodies were removed. Alli asked some routine questions and agreed to show up. As she hung up the phone all she could think to say was "Damn!"

When she arrived at the victims residence, the first thing she noticed was the officers had that certain look about them. You know, the thousand yard stare. Or the look they would get when they found dead kids. Angry, but frightened. She was met by Detective Tim Renolds. A ten year veteran with a military background. He escorted FBI Chapman into the house. There was the first victim. A young white male in his twenties. His body was face down, but his head was twisted around backward. His arms were out away from his body. It was horrific and hard to look at.

"Excuse me agent, but have you ever seen a body displayed like this?" She did not respond. Instead she bent down noticing very little blood loss. A little from the mouth, but she thought there should be more. The head twisting was violent. Certainly with this injury there would be blood in the eyes, nose, or both. "Have you collected for DNA" Alli stood and faced the detective.

"Yes. I've got our CSI investigators on it. They're sampling all three victims. Collecting fluids, dusting for prints. Both inside and outside the crime scenes. There's not much blood and nothing seems to be out of place. There were some smudge marks on the kitchen floor. As if someone was dragged. We took pictures."

FBI Chapman walked around the body making mental notes. Detective Renolds watched her as she studied the crime scene. She was beautiful. Brown hair pulled back in a ponytail. Black jeans and a leather coat. FBI Chapman packed a semi-automatic on her right. Partially covered by her coat. She had on occasion used it. Detective Renolds noticed something else about her. She seemed to have a great deal of compassion for the victim. The look on her face while she worked. How gentle she was when physically examining the body. If she needed to adjust the victim for any reason, she was gentle and deliberate. Moving the boys arm, she cradled it until gently returning to it's original position. When it seemed like she had paused in her examination, Detective Renolds added some detail.

"What's really weird is the other two victims are exactly like this one. It's like they're mirror images of one another." For a moment Alli stared at the detective. It was the first time she made real eye contact with him. "Mirror image." He repeated.

"I would like to go see them now." FBI Chapman was direct. The two detectives left together and drove to the other crime scenes. Another residence, and an alley way in Tempe, by Arizona State University. One male victim the other a female student. Both displayed exactly like the first victim. Agent Chapman immediately recognized these murders fit the qualifications for serial killings. But she knew to keep quiet. She could write what she wanted in her report, but saying the words this early in the investigation was a political nightmare. The Phoenix cops had already figured it out. They were not about to say a word.

In the alley way near Arizona State University the Medical Examiner arrived. He had already been to the residence of the third victim. As soon as his driver exited the truck, he saw the dead girl. He began to pray. He backed away and leaned on the vehicle. His boss tried to settle him down, but the man was in tears.

"Have you ever seen anything like this? I can't be here. This is evil! I have to leave." After a few moments of eye contact with the Medical Examiner, his assistant returned to the truck. He sat with his head down. Today would be his last working for the Medical Examiners office. Of course no one had seen deaths like these. They were awful murders. And the staged remains were inexplicable. It gave Allison a terrible gut feeling. She wondered if there was something new out there. Some new way to kill. Staring at the poor girl with her head turned around, Alli began whispering. It helped her analyze and remember details. Finally she pulled the detective aside.

"You were right. They're identical. Too close to be a coincidence. Too perfect. What's going on here?" Detective Renolds did not respond. Everyone that witnessed the bodies was deeply affected. Some more than others. The detective would be happy if the FBI would take over. He tried not to show it, but he was frightened.

Eighty-five hundred miles away in Bangkok, Thailand, their police detective was beginning his examination of the first of three bodies. All with their heads turned all the way around.

Chapter 3

A few days after examining the crime scenes, Alli got a call from the Maricopa County medical examiner. They requested that she, along with a representative of the Phoenix police department, come down to the morgue. Autopsies and DNA results were ready and there were some extraordinary discoveries. Some that truly puzzled the coroner. When Alli arrived, there were three bodies on three tables. Still frozen in their position of death. They had been reversed so they could be examined. Their heads turned to the side. The medical examiner walked from table to table as he began his briefing.

"The necks of the three victims were broken in a precise manner. Right down to the same vertebrae. They were reversed at exactly the same angle, meaning the same amount of torque was used to achieve the effect. And of most interest to me, red blood cells within each body have exploded. Not all, but enough that I would think they underwent some form of shock, or stunning!"

"So somebody shocked them first, then broke their necks?" Alli asked.

"Possibly," the examiner responded. "But I've never seen this type of cellular disintegration before. It's almost mechanical. Precise somehow."

"What kind of stun gun does that? Is there something new on the market?" Alli was looking for answers.

Standing around the autopsy table they discussed this and other factors, but the real concerns were two fold. Did these murders qualify as serial? Certainly three murders were enough. And how was the killer so precise? Someone had to be very strong to turn the heads around. However, there was no hemorrhaging in the eyes, a sure sign of choking. No bruising around the neck where the killer would have placed his or her hands. So how were the heads twisted and the bodies staged?

The FBI agent had other questions that for the moment she kept to herself. Like why were these individuals singled out? What made them special enough, the killer chose them? The medical examiner added he thought the guy was a creep because he laid his kills out so precisely. Displaying them with no respect. Pulling their arms out to the side, and pushing their eyelids back. Generally displaying them in a taunting, unflattering way. Alli Chapman agreed with him.

"Do you think this guy is trying to make a statement, Doctor? Is he one of these that likes to taunt authority?" Her questions were valid. Examining the killer's method and the result, told Alli she was in for a hell of a ride. This case was not ordinary. She felt revulsion. How could any human being do this to another?

Detective Renolds failed to make the Medical Examiners meeting, so Alli called him and they met at a midtown coffee hangout. When they both arrived, she filled him in. But there was little to explain how the victims could be connected. Nothing to detour this case from the weird. It was creepy. Outside of phisical details, the medical examination only added more questions. No common threads between the victims. And cursory computer inquires for related crimes, fell short. There were none. The victims seemed random.

After finishing her coffee, Alli attempted to change the subject.

"Did I understand correctly? You were in the military?"

"Yes." He said. "I was a Staff Sergeant in the Iraq War. And no, I don't think these murders have a military signature."

"You don't think so?" She asked. "I kinda wondered." His explanation left no doubt.

"Common strangle hold technique leaves a tell-tail bruise. It's just not likely that someone with that training did this." The detective raised his coffee cup, but before he took a sip. "And if you don't mind me asking agent Chapman, what's the motive here? This looks like killing for pleasure. Random victims the SOB ran across. Wrong place at the wrong time."

Alli thought his scenario was relatively sound except for one of her nagging questions. Why would anybody go to so much trouble staging the victims? It must have taken time. If there was a new stun gun out there, it would explain a lot. But neither investigator knew of anything that would contort bodies like that.

"What are we missing here, Tim? This guy kills in public. He's obviously not worried about being caught."

"Well FBI agent Allison Chapman, if he's just getting started he will make mistakes. We'll get him!" It was a nice thought from the detective. But it would soon be amended.

Chapter 4

A month went by. No other murders. None locally. Not the uncommon type anyway. There were no new leads. No one claiming responsibility, and Alli had other duties. Her boss constantly bragged that she was a great investigator. He kept her running all over the southwest. Then one day she got a call from her detective. Detective Tim. She had begun calling him that in recent weeks. They had become friends. Mostly over the phone. But they enjoyed each others company. The occasional drinks and dinner had become a regular thing. But she had never heard Tim like this. He was very excited about something.

"You're not going to believe what I found. Go on line. Find the Bangkok, Thailand police web site. Click on homicide investigations." Alli did what he instructed. There it was. The Bangkok authorities own notes on three murders that took place in one day. The same day as the Phoenix murders.

"Unbelievable." She said. As she read on, Tim read-her in on background, over the phone.

"I don't know how I could have missed this, Alli. But we know it now, damn it!" He was almost screaming.

"Does anyone else know?" She asked. "I mean have you told anyone else about this?"

"No. It's too weird. I came across it last night, and haven't slept since. I almost called you. But I didn't know what your schedule looked like. I didn't want to keep you awake." He continued.

"How can there be simultaneous events, with the same M.O., on opposite sides of the Earth? It's crazy! It doesn't make sense unless there's more than one killer."

Alli had a hard time formulating words. This was extraordinary. After a brief silence, she spoke up.

"I wonder if the Bangkok police know about our murders?"

"I don't know, Alli. But our investigation is on line for all to read. It's just a matter of time. This is going to freak a lot of people out."

"What do you think, Tim? Should we contact Bangkok or talk to our bosses first?"

"Probably the later, but lets sleep on it. I'm ready for a drink. Can you meet me at "The Rose?" Alli thought about it for two seconds. "Absa- freaking-lootly!" The Rose was a downtown bar. A lot of cops made it their off duty spot. After a couple drinks it became clear that the Bangkok discovery needed to be aired. Alli and Tim agreed to call for a meeting in the morning. They would explain to all what they had found.

Sometimes humans make great progress. This was not one of those times. After the meeting with muc-e-mucs from every department of American security in the known universe, it was determined that more unexplained murders had taken place. A lot more. With the same M.O. Alli and Tim had not been told. Connections were not made. Truth had been withheld. In some cases police kept things quiet out of fear. Strange triple homicides might bring negative fallout for their communities.

Alli stood as if to walk out. Her disgust clearly visible. Her boss, an Assistant Director waved her back.

"Agent Chapman, please stay. Return to your seat and I promise we'll get to the bottom of this." He attempted a look of support.

"Excuse me." A tall, thin, elderly gentleman stood to take the floor.

"We have decided one thing. In an earlier, closed door meeting, we decided on a name for this killer. We have chosen, "The Phoenix/Bangkok Phenomenon." Alli's eyes went bright red as she stared at Tim. He immediately spoke up.

"What's this? Is this in honor of Alli's and my work? Please. So there are murders taking place all over the world, and we should capitalize on that? This is a very dangerous situation we are in. We're way behind on this case and it's looking quite anomalous." He turned so he could face the entire room. "Not to mention Alli and I are thinking the same thing. Two words. Scape and Goat. We need to be damn careful with this."

There were a few moments of silence, but the FBI director had already decided on a course of action. People around the world were beginning to take notice. The press had received stories. When they get involved, decisions are made based on politics. To the press and the establishment, this was sizing up to be the murder story of the century.

Allison was furious. She couldn't help but mimic the press.

"Unexplained deaths everywhere! What is happening? Oh no..." Her boss from the Phoenix bureau looked her way.

"That's enough Alli. I understand how you feel, but this isn't the time for that. Here's a case file for you and Detective Renolds. It's the same M.O. in Austin. Grab a jet and interview the police and a family. The daughter was the only survivor of an attack. It looks like our guy. And by the way, the name we came up with is not a coincidence. You two are working together. You both, were first on the case. So go do your job."

The detectives left without a word. The top brass had spoke. That was that. No rebuke. The press was involved. That got things moving.

That's right. The press was involved. With all it's glory. Usually in the wrong direction. Twisting the truth. Or, just making things up. Entertaining. But not what America signed up for.

The local Phoenix stations had originally mentioned the murders. But it was Phoenix after all. Murders, even strange ones, did occur. So at first the reporting was a bit benign. But now... It was unreal. Like someone lit a fuse. Every major media outlet reported 24/7. The Phenomenon murders were the talk of cable news. People were dying. Three at a time. The dead were adding up fast. By Tim's calculation, the death toll could be nearing one thousand, world wide. He left the early morning meeting, overly upset.

"Listening to those people drives me nuts. They may be our superiors, but they're going to screw this up. I rechecked the internet, Alli. It's already full of crap. People are just making thing up. The only legitimate investigation is in Bangkok. But they don't have a witness. Neither do we. There are no damn witnesses! They held out on us. You're the only one I trust."

The duo were not given the facts. They sat idle for a month. While the killer or killers continued their spree. They were angry! Neither knew who to trust. Except each other.

Chapter 5

After landing in Austin, the agents set up shop at the local bureau office. They were given a room, and interview times were set up with the Travis County Sheriffs office. Anyone directly involved with the Bower Ranch incident was asked to come in.

The Sheriffs department's notes and verbal description of the crime scene left no doubt. It was the same as Phoenix. Three gruesome murders. Bodies staged in a frightening pose. An officer's body-cam clearly showed each victim. Heads turned all the way around. Arms out to the side. However, in the months following the attack, there were no new leads. Travis County was stuck. After the interviews, one officer asked to speak to Tim privately. They stepped into the hall where he felt comfortable.

"Sir, I thought you should hear this off the record. One of the victims at that tail gate was the daughter of a local politician. He didn't want any Death-by-Strange-Nature talk. If you know what I mean. He even tried to get our Medical Examiner to change some paper work that ruled Unusual Death. After that, one of our Detectives went to talk to him. He told him to stop doing what he was doing. The politician tried hitting him with a club. He was arrested and went to jail. Now everybody feels sorry for this guy. He lost his kid and everything, but you can't be hitting on one of us. The press wrote salacious lies about his daughter anyway."

"Ya, I'll bet they did." Tim replied. "Thanks for confiding. Do you mind me telling this story to my partner?"

"No. I just felt more comfortable out here." The officer left and Tim went back inside. He relayed the story to Alli. She promptly looked it up on her lap top. The politician was fined and released as fast as he was arrested. In his statement to the police, he mentioned that his daughter was not suppose to be at the Bowers. She had gone there to meet a boy her father didn't approve of.

Alli closed her lap top and stood up.

"You know Tim, all these cops sounded alike. Almost apologetic. Like they were sorry for not knowing more. Or tell us more. So we can capture this guy. Or guys. But the cops are scared. Every one of them. They don't want to know any more. They're all scared to death."

Like usual Tim Renolds was amazed at Alli's observational skills. He had seen something in their behavior as well. But he never would have seen what was behind their eyes. Not the way she did. Anyone that was read in on this case, was scared. Nothing fit. It all seemed impossible.

Tim and Alli drove to the Bower Ranch to get a statement from Kate Lynn and her parents. They had called for an appointment and the Bowers agreed. Though they did not feel they had any additional information to give.

When they arrived, they were met by a long well maintained driveway, leading to a beautiful single level, traditional Texas ranch house. After the introductions, the investigators were seated on a custom couch. Surrounded by hand made furniture. In one corner, Alli noticed a grand piano. It brought back memories of her youth and her own musical education. She thought the home was beautiful.

After a bit of guarded silence, Alli gently broke in. She read the room pretty well. No hard questions.

"The workman in overalls. It was reported that no one saw them again. Did you actually see them leave the meadow?" Alli was gentle with Kate Lynn. She could tell it had been rough. She was snuggled up with her mother on the opposing couch.

"I don't remember." She said softly. "The police have been looking for them." At that point, Mrs. Bower spoke up.

"The police put out a, oh, you know. What do you call it? A Bolo?"

"Yes, mam. A be-on-the-lookout." Alli chimed. "It means to watch for someone."

"Yes. Well, that's all we know." Mrs. Bower continued. "They never said what company the men worked for, and we never asked."

"I don't think they know." Alli responded.

"Sometimes electric company people are on our land. It's got lines running straight through it. It's a fare spread. About a square mile." Mr. Bower was obviously proud of his place.

"Kate, we are very sorry for your loss. We were told you were very close to your boyfriend. Detective Renolds and I understand how hard this has been for you."

Alli stood to leave. It took Tim by surprise. He still had questions for the family. But he followed Alli's lead and stood as well.

"I don't believe we have any more questions for you or your family. It was a pleasure to meet all of you." Alli said. Tim said good by as well and they prepared to drive back to town. When they got outside, Tim gently took Alli's arm. Mr. Bower had two men following them. Not threatening. But present. When the reached their rental, Tim whispered in Alli's ear. The two man escort changed the circumstance of the meeting.

"I want to go back in there. Until Bower sent those two out here, I was ready to leave. Now I want to press that young woman. Why doesn't she remember the men in overalls? I'm holding a report that says they walked in front of Buddy's truck. It's her deposition. She clearly saw men in overalls. I want to know who they are."

"I know, Tim. People with head trauma remember more than this gal. She's blocking. I don't think it's her fault. Get in the car. I want to tell you a story." As the detectives drove down the driveway, Tim could see Bowers' men in the rear view mirror. Also, Mr. Bower had joined them.

It would be easy for Alli Chapman to right off Kate Lynn as just a victim. She was a victim. She was a victim twice. Once as the sole survivor of a horrific crime. The second time at the hands of her parents.

"I've seen this before. Notice how Kate's mom and dad kept finishing the story? They forced her to forget. She told them what happened that night. All the gory details. She probably had nightmares every night. I'd go so far as to say they may have hired someone. A psychologist to help scrub her head. She's tainted. Nothing is real to that chic. Buddy's gone. She's just living in a fantasy now. She's their little angel. The rich folks don't want their little girl screwed up for life."

"Ok." Tim replied. "That's pretty convincing. I realize it doesn't matter what she remembers. I'm just trying to be thorough. I still want to know who the damn men were. They could have been the killers. I keep thinking about the bodies. I hate like hell saying this, but you and I know there's nothing on Earth that can do that do somebody. Identical deformed bodies everywhere. That's impossible."

"Then what are you suggesting, detective? Are you sure you want to go down that path? I've already done it."

"Damn it, Alli. Let me put it like this. Remember Occam's Razor? If there's two ways to solve something, the simplest is probably correct. I don't like where this is going."

Alli smiled a big beautiful smile. She did that periodically. She didn't like where the case was going either. For law enforcement types, words like unexplained were never good. Certain words or phrases, complicated things.

"Tim, there's always the possibility of the supernatural. Some things can't be explained. Especially if you believe it."

It was time to return to Phoenix. If they were lucky, the bosses would not call. Maybe they could turn the case over to someone else.

Chapter 6

"Alli, Alli wake up!" She was draped over her desk. Someone put her leather coat over her shoulders while she slept. "What time?" She moaned.

"It's six o'clock, PM! You've been sleeping for three hours and a couple of times there were so many people in here, I thought you might wake up. You didn't so I let you sleep."

"Oh." She gave Tim A big sleepy grin. He watched her for a few moments before dropping a bomb.

"Some things have been going on around here you might like to know about." Allison closed her eyes again. She was not asleep, and Tim saw that she still had a big smile on her face.

"Alli, hold on to your seat. There's a really strange story coming out of England. It's almost as weird as our case." Alli swiveled back and forth in her chair, her head resting on the desk. "Alli," Tim was almost whispering. "Two witnesses claim they saw a young woman floating." Alli's eyes popped open. "Yes, floating! Just above the ground."

"What! Screw that!" Alli Chapman was awake now. She stood up and glared at Tim as if he were messing with here.

"Ya, I know, but it gets better. She floats into a home in the country. A family driving down the road sees this, chases her into the home and guess what they found. Three dead!"

"No way! NO WAY! Come on Tim, that's crap! I'll bet you found that on the internet!"

"You're funny," he replied. "NO, it's on official Interpol Email. We received it while you slept. It was sent all over the world. A lot of agencies have read this. Most are dismissing it. Do you want to hear the rest?"

"There's more? I got all this education for this?" Detective Tim tried not to laugh out loud at his partner.

"They didn't find the girl in the house. She had all ready left. They did find her victims, assuming she did it." Alli just shook her head in disbelief.

"I've seen a lot of things doing this job. Some of which are damn strange. That's the weirdest thing I've ever heard. You don't believe it, do you?"

"Alli, we are working an incredibly strange case. Can't you feel it in your gut? We need to check this out. At least interview the witnesses for credibility."

"To London? You want me to go to London? I don't know Tim. I've been on the move for the Phoenix office quite a bit lately. Plus our trip to Austin. I'd like to stay home. I know this case is weird and I probably should go with you, but I need a break."

"Ya, I know. This case is insane. Keep an eye on things here. I'll see you in a few days."

"Thanks Tim. Be safe."

"I'll bring you back a Bobby!" Alli smiled as Tim headed out. Driving to the airport he could not shake the one word Alli used to describe their case. Weird! The whole thing was weird. "The Phenoenon." This story from England. The Interpol Email was very strange. Not the usual police notification. The event described in the Email must have been vetted to a certain extent. Someone thought it was real enough to release. That made Tim very nervous. If true, it moved the investigation toward the supernatural. It opened the door for the press, and the internet. To make up whatever they wanted. He worried. News like this would trivialize the murders. The press would love it. Tim hit the steering wheel with his fist. "I can hear it now....Floating woman kills again! My alien ate my homework! Damn press." He really wished Alli had come along. He really liked working with her. She was damn smart and read people well.

Law enforcement types learn to do that. But Alli had natural instincts. A quality that can not be taught. He noticed something else about his partner. When he walked into a room full of people and Alli was present, she stood out. It did not matter where. His office, her office, a press briefing. Allison stood out. It wasn't something he could put a finger on. She always looked different than everyone else in the room. It wasn't just her beauty. She belonged somewhere.

In an apartment in London, a beautiful young girl kissed her father good night. She did not remember what she had done the night before. Her mind was wiped clean. Just like a girl in Texas. Just like so many others. She always got good grades and was popular in school. She planned to go to college and would soon leave home. She was the girl next door.

Her memory loss was an effect. It was not her doing. The British girl would never know what happened. She would only know the love of her family. As their daughter climbed the stairs to her bedroom, her father gazed at her mother. "Our little girl, how beautiful she's become."

Chapter 7 History

Throughout Europe, Eastern Asia, and as far south as Northern Africa, the Plague caused unbelievable death and suffering. Along with out of work soldiers back from the Crusades, two thirds of the regions population disappeared. It diminished from ninety-million to thirty-million in a relatively short period of time.

The spiritual conversation was that God was angry and he chose that moment in time to cleanse the Earth. Demons were released to enter the body, leaving terrible scares before death. The truth is, the Plague is the Plague. It kills. As far as the Crusaders were concerned, they were just bored. They had nothing else to do. The Crusades were over. No more fortune and glory. It is hard to imagine that roving marauders could add so significantly to the continental death toll. However, rape, riches, and land were excellent incentives. Out of work soldiers traveling from town to hamlet. Leaving nothing behind.

History is replete with genocidal chapters. There will always be a virus for our scientists to battle. It seems mankind keeps creating new illnesses. Just the fact we group together must contribute to our fragility. One thing our society must do is remain watchful of our country and the world. There are always individuals trying to destroy the rest of us for their own gain. We must identify them. Prevent them from coming to power. For if we don't, we will pay a heavy price.

It has also been said that as far as intelligent life goes, we are on top of the food chain. Kings of all we see. We even travel outside our own atmosphere, and stare back at our domain. Incredible technology. Only accomplished in the last one hundred years. But what if we're not alone? What if we share the Earth with a species of equal intelligence? Some argue that many animals have proven time and time again that they are as smart as we are. No, even if we share the planet we must still be kings.

Jules Verne hypothesized that there is life underground, and anyone can reach the "Center of the Earth." You just had to know how to get there.

Chapter 8

Alli stood on the sidewalk taking photos of her Phoenix home. It was watering day on her block. A monthly ritual she looked forward to. It was the day different varieties of cactus extended their lives thanks to her generosity. It had been a productive morning. Alli planted a new Yucca, finishing it off with a drink from the hose. There were other cactus she called by name. Dubbed when she was a child. They too waited for a drink. A drink of the rarest substance in the desert. It was a beautiful morning. The best time to do anything in the desert. Alli like to ride her bike in the early dawn hours. She loved to watch the Sun rise and see the desert turn from black to gold. Shadows from the Saguaros proved their human quality. Alli thought they looked like thousands of people. She had a large Saguaro in her front yard. It was left over from when the house was built. Alli inherited the house from her father. She knew she would never leave. However, the Saguaro was looking a bit ragged. It was very old.

She continued taking photographs when something caught her eye. A flash off to the right of the driveway. She instinctively reached for her weapon, but it was inside her house. Alli walked diagonally across the drive. When out of no where stood a man.!

"What, who are you? Where did you come from?" Alli started toward the front door. Weapon and cell phone, she thought.

"My name is not important. You are Allison Chapman." Now she ran to the door. This guy knows my name. Am I being set up? "Mr. who are you?" She asked sternly. "I don't have time for any bull!"

"Please Miss Chapman, you don't know me but I've come a long way to meet you. Please don't be afraid. Let me explain."

"Ok, you wait right here!" She ran in, grabbed her automatic, checked the magazine, loaded it up and went straight out to greet him!

"Dude, where did you come from?" Alli raised her weapon as she spoke. "I would have seen you walking down the street. My yard is secure in back, so how did you sneak up on me?"

"I can't tell you my name, but you are FBI agent Allison Chapman and you like to explore caves."

"So you know a little bit about me. You still shouldn't sneak up on people. It can get you killed!"

"Please Miss Chapman, may we go inside and talk? What I have to say is very important, and time, for you, is running out. I mean you no harm." Something told Alli it was all right, but to keep the gun at her side. They entered the house, and once inside the visitor said, "What I'm about to tell you is going to change a lot of lives. Murders are taking place all over the world and I believe I can help."

Alli went into shock. "What did you say? What do you know about that?" She raised her weapon again. This dude is weird, she thought. The man raised one hand. As it taking an oath.

"To help you, two things need to happen. I need to tell you a story and you have to come with me. You must see for yourself." Alli studied the man for a moment, then lowering her gun she asked him to sit down. As she was doing the same he began his tale.

"I come from a great city." He paused, unsure she was prepared for what he was about to say. "My home is buried deep in the Earth's crust!" Alli wanted to laugh, but something kept here quiet. The way he was dressed. A long coat in such hot weather. His pants and shoes. She had not seen anything quite like them. His skin color was very pale. Caucasian, but pale. As if not enough Sun.

"We don't appear on the surface at all. You are our first contact with the surface in a very long time."

Something ominous came over Alli. She felt the gut wrenching dig of reality setting in. That everything she knew to be the truth about her life, was about to be altered forever. The problem was, she was beginning to believe. How could she not? Supernatural murders and this guy says he's from under the ground? It was not too hard to make the connection.

The man told Alli about his home. How beautiful it was. With massive buildings and many species of plant flora that thrived.

"It's a wonderful place Allison, but something has happened. Something we didn't expect. You must come with me. We need you to understand." Alli sat back in her chair.

"How could this be?" She thought. "How is it that no one knows about them?" "This is impossible!" She said out loud. For a moment there was silence. The pale gentleman smiled. He tried to reassure her. He understood what she was going through. But knew her intelligence would help with the transition. Coming to her was no accident. She had already been vetted.

Alli bent over holding her stomach. Then put her head in her hands. Then in one motion threw her hair back over her head. She felt a little sick, but realized this was very important. She stared at him for a moment.

"Allison, you must trust me. This is all real."

In that moment she realized she'd been waiting for this her whole life. She continued to stare, but now she was grinning.

Millions of miles away, six beings from inside the Earths' crust travel to observe Jupiter's Red spot. An incredible storm that surface dwelling humans can only see by sending a satellite or looking through a telescope. The travelers home is deep within the Earth. They don't experience storms, so it is a real curiosity. They are very advanced and travel to locations that teach about nature and the universe. But they do not share with humans on the surface. In fact there is no interaction at all. This was decided fifteen thousand years before the Wright brothers flew their airplane.

The truth is, that within the millions of years life has been evolving on Earth, civilizations could have come and gone and we would know nothing about it. Scientists believe the Dinosaurs died out about sixty-five million years ago. That's like saying the distance from your shoulder to the end of your finger tips represents the age of the Earth. About six billion years. The dinosaurs lived about where your wrist is. We would be at your finger tips. So what about all the time in between?

We created our way of keeping time. Days, years... clocks, hour glasses. But we really don't understand it.

Chapter 9

"Ok! I'll go. I'll go with you." She felt like throwing up.

"I admit, I'm frightened. There's nothing in the FBI manual that prepares you for this."

"Allison, you are very brave. You will learn what this is about soon. Be strong. Your strength is one of the reasons we came for you."

"I don't feel very strong right now. This is so weird." She wished Tim was there. This could blow the case wide open.

"How does this work?" She asked.

"Just walk toward me." Allis' legs were like lead, but she followed his directions and advanced.

"Take my hand." She reached out, and with her first step she stopped. "OH, my God!"

In an instant Alli and her companion transported to his home. Her eyes adjusted in seconds and she realized she was standing on a cliff staring at the most incredible sight she had ever seen. A city of immense size laid out in front of them for miles. It could have been any large city except for the fact it was in a cave under the crust of the Earth! Her guides description had not done it justice. It was beautiful!

There was light. It was low and throughout the massive cavern. Alli felt a little frightened. "I'm on a different world," she whispered.

"Are you alright, Allison?" He was clutching her arm.

"I'm not sure. What happened?"

"We have arrived at my home. We have arrived at Granitaria!"

For several moments the two travelers looked out over the cliff. The pale man remained quiet while Alli took it all in. "How did we get here?" She asked.

"My people have mastered the ability to move through the Earth. We found it was necessary if we were to remain inside."

"We needed to be able to move through solid rock. This is achieved by generating pathways that reduce matter to a particle stream. Thus we may travel on them much like your highways. They are limited in number so we move them to suit our needs. We call it particle boring."

The pale man escorted Alli down a beautifully manicured path. It lead down from the cliff to the floor of the cavern. They were immediately met by fields of assorted vegetables, and one field that looked like moss. The kind you would see in your yard. Bright green and fluffy. It was lovely. The colors were incredible. From the cavern to the buildings, to the fields and orchards. There were lots of them. What looked like apples, but different in color. More purple than red or green. "Incredible." She said. "Is this real?" The man with no name, she trusted with her life, went on to explain their history.

"Our evolution took place at the same time as yours. As we evolved, we stayed in the caves. When your ancestors walked out of the caves we went further in. Moving rock, digging tunnels. A lot of us died. Eventually, moving farther underground we discovered this place. We call it Granitaria!"

"Granitaria? It's beautiful!" Alli's Adrenaline level was beginning to subside.

"Are you feeling better? We still have a bit of a walk."

"Yes," she said. "Why don't we know about you? You're humans. Why wait so long to contact us?"

"Allison, all will be reveled. Look upon the next few hours like a vacation. Let me show you my home." For the next few minutes her guide revealed the Granitarian past "In the beginning we used fire for warmth. We scrounged for food and protected our young. As we grew, we developed heat for our homes. It's very rare that we need it. The cavern remains at a constant seventy-five degrees. On occasion though it will get cold here. We developed industry, machinery and sciences. Education has always been important, and we developed quickly. One of our greatest achievements is a type of never ending light. It gives us sight in the darkness and seasons to plant by. Something we lost when we gave up the surface."

They stopped on the far side of one of the orchards. Though they had to walk a little further, detail of the main buildings was becoming clearer. Alli raised her arms out in front of her. "Look at this place! It's magnificent!"

"Allison, welcome to Granitaria!"

She was close enough to see the difference in architecture. There was nothing like this on the surface. The buildings were tall and slender. Bathed in light. More modern. More futuristic. Inside she could see figures moving. Thousands of people living their lives.

"I can see them. Through the windows!"

"No!" her guide said, "Our buildings don't have windows. The sides are cut crystal. It is our primary building material. We cut it so precisely, you can see through it."

"Oh, my." Alli was close to tears.

She saw what looked like an airport. It had hangers, and disc shaped craft parked along a runway. There were different shapes and sizes. She pointed, as she nervously asked the question.

"Is that what I think it is?"

"We are an advanced civilization by surface standards. Our space craft travel very fast! There are openings in the Earths' crust when we want to leave."

"Sometimes you accidentally see one of our craft. That has been going on since your middle ages. Before that, very rarely did we venture up. Though recently we had occasion to send out a search party. But we'll get to that later. Once in a while, one of our explorers climbs to the surface. For you it would be like climbing a mountain, but our people never contact anyone from the surface. We only study you and report your historical events to our people."

Study us? Alli felt that statement was odd. But not threatening. Also, she wondered who they were searching for.

"Where are we?" Alli tried to relate by asking questions she thought he would answer. "Where are we in relation to the surface?"

"I can't tell you that. Not yet. Maybe in the future, but not now. We have rules here in Granitaria. You would compare them to your laws. Ours, however, are simple. Our people accept them from the time they are born. First, everyone's life is precious. So only natural or accidental death is permitted. This rule has only been broken once. That individual was taken very far away. The second rule is, our home is Granitaria. It can be a hostile environment. So we must always help one another survive."

At that point, Alli felt she had to ask. "Are there earthquakes here?"

"No. Not life threatening ones. We feel minor tremors, but this cavern has been here for millions of years. If your wondering about rule number two, remember, these rules were designed thousands of years ago. They've never been changed. This was and still is a hostile environment." Alli thought about the United States. How the laws she protected as an FBI agent were only a few hundred years old. It help put things in perspective. Her guide continued.

"The third rule is our children are most important. Our future depends on them. We never reveal our location and we never bring surface dwelling humans to Granitaria. So you see Allison, we feel you are very special. You have a certain "skill set." Your position in life, one of authority, makes you perfect for this unusual partnership. Trust, as you can see from our rules, is very important to us. And very important to this situation. We can't just go to your leaders. It wouldn't come out well. We don't trust them."

Like stepping off a space ship onto a new planet. Being the first outsider to see the new world. FBI agent Alli Chapman was overwhelmed! This was a lot to take in. It was obvious they thought she was of value. But what if that were to change? It was a risk that she was willing to take. Granitarian technology was far superior. That alone was worth the trip. She told herself to remember everything she saw. She may never be allowed to come here again.

Chapter 10

On the surface, the murders continued. No matter the political climate, all the countries of the world joined in a conscious collective of fear. Fear of the unknown. Even if two or more countries were at war with conventional weapons, "The Phenomenon" effect scared people more. It was a plague that science could not cure. Some believed it was a virus that killed in a manor never seen before. But scientists claimed there was no evidence of that at all. Doctors could not help the living, only observe the dead. This was a law enforcement issue and the world prayed for it to end.

The number of dead added up quickly. With the exception of a sensationalized report coming out of London, there was nothing to go on. Most authorities did not believe the "floating girl" story anyway. It was dismissed as just fear mongering to explain away "The Phenomenon." Detective Tim returned with his sealed report. He wanted to talk to Alli before his boss got a hold of it. What he found in London was interesting and dangerous. He wanted Alli to review the statements with him. Make sure it was safe to release. Some of the statements were very provocative. He tried calling her, but she did not answer. He called several times, but got the same result. Tim was worried. It was not like her. She always took his calls. He guessed she was in the middle of something very important. When he got to the station, his boss Captain P.J. Sweet pulled Tim into his office. "Boy, you've got some problems." He handed Tim a London newspaper that quoted him talking about a "Floating Girl," and that he believed the story to be true.

"I didn't talk to any papers! One of the Bobbies talked. That's the only explanation. No one read my report."

Captain Sweet went on to explain that the Mayor's office received calls from Washington. The news of one of their own talking to the British press had the political types thrashing their offices and screaming to the gods! Words like international incident were being thrown about, but Tim was never called in. This was not about him.

It was about a bunch of very scared politicians. Way in over their heads. Tim was furious that his name had been used, but Sweet calmed him down by turning on a T.V. The network news media had politicians and clergy on every channel. Trying to reassure the people. A community organizer/ self proclaimed minister speaking sympathetically, holding his hands out in front of him and reminding his flock that the living must honor the dead. Meanwhile, his aids looked for ways to exploit "The Phenomenon." Behavior seen many times in recent years.

Though he wished he could have consulted with Alli first, he revealed to his boss that the Brit originally interviewing the two witnesses, immediately quit! No explanation. Tim felt this added to the credibility of their story. "Boss, Scotland Yard was really nervous while I was there. True or not, the "floating girl" story is damn weird." Privately, Tim was sure it was connected to their investigation. The witnesses stuck by their story.

People tried to go on with their lives, but it was scary out there. Mothers stayed home with their kids, but if the Grim Reaper came, he came. No one was immune. Fathers would leave for work and not return. Only to be found later. Bodies face down. Their heads turned one-hundred-eighty-degrees. Arms out to their sides. Families came together. Kids living on their own came home to their parents. No one ever walked to their cars alone. But that didn't matter. There was the standard run on groceries. All over the world people prepared themselves for something terrible.

The current climate in Washington, stoked the sales of handguns. The more talk of gun control, the more guns were sold. "The Phenomenon" doubled sales. People wanted to protect their families. When scientists discovered three sets of bodies in Antarctica, the news sealed the publics view of the killer. He could reach anyone. He was a monster.

It was a dark time. People heard their neighbors scream in the night. Those same people no longer trusted their neighbors.

Chapter 11

Alli and her guide walked side by side toward the city. At one point they stopped to rest. Her host removed a soft sided pouch from under his coat.

"Drink Allison. It's water." She was happy to and thought it tasted delicious.

Looking forward, Alli realized there was a wall of brush in front of them. The path they walked lead straight into the foliage. They continued and soon it became clear that what looked like brush, were actually trees. The trees were not tall. Ten or twelve feet and were planted so close together, they resembled tall shrubs. Thousands of them.

Looking left of the path, then right, Alli could not see where the trees ended. Only an arched walk way to pass through. The trees there had been trained to form an arch spanning the width of the path.

"It looks kind of dark in there."

"Come Allison, you'll be all right."

AS they entered the tree line, a soft, white light enveloped the path. Not bright, just enough light to see their way. When they emerged, Alli and her guide stood at the edge of the city.

Alli was a cave explorer. In recent years she visited Tennessee with some of her FBI colleagues. With many caves in Tennessee to choose from, their spelunking trip was a lot of fun. When she was young, her father introduced her to caving in Arizona. But Granitaria was overwhelming. She calculated the width of the cavern at over a mile. But there was no way to determine the length. The ceiling was hundreds of feet high. The buildings were many stories as well. The structures went on forever.

The residents were known as Granitarians, and as Alli Chapman walked further in, she met some of them. Some took no notice of her at all. While others looked at her and smiled. Everyone was pale and wore overalls. Or some type of one piece, multicolored jump suit.

Large stalactites hung from the ceiling. Some hundreds of feet long. Alli thought it looked like the Redwood forest hanging up side down.

Stalagmites came up from the spaces between the buildings. Everywhere a soft yellow light permeated the cave. All of Granitaria seemed to be laid out in perfect harmony with the natural cavern.

Alli saw immediately why people had never left. They found peace.

"Allison, that building there is where your apartment is. We have prepared it for you, and a woman is there to assist you with anything you need. Over there is where you will meet with our people to discuss why you are here."

Alli took note of the open air complex. For a moment, Alli and her guide stood in front of her building. As if in sync, using all their senses. They took in the city. Lost time mixed with humility, swept over her. She almost forgot about the terrible death on the surface. She looked up as if to see straight though to her home. Past the massive pillars. Through miles of rock. She saw home. Why couldn't it be like this? Divest of terrible acts of violence. If this cavern had once been a hostile environment, the Granitarians had made it warm and inviting. She felt protected here. Safe. Like never before in her life.

They flew upwards in an elevator that seemed to move on a cloud. Exiting, they followed a hallway then entered an apartment where a woman stood to greet them. "Please Allison, don't ask her name. That's all we ask of you while you are here. Until you understand the problem we have, we must remain anonymous."

The apartment was one room. A large couch sat at the foot of the clear crystal wall. But when the woman waved her hand over the front edge of the couch, it transformed into a bed! "When you are ready for sleep, think the wall dark. It will frost and give you added security." The soft spoken woman had gentle, beautiful eyes. Alli trusted her immediately. There was, what could only be called a toilet. On the opposite wall it was square and sat near the ice box. Pointing at it the woman said, "Yes, we need to refrigerate our food just like you!" With that she put her hand over her mouth and both women giggled. "This is a dream!" Alli said out loud. "It must be a dream."

Chapter 12 Revelation

"He has betrayed all of us!" A strong male voice carried throughout the open air complex. Precise engineering allowed sound to carry throughout the city. There was no need for a public address system. Hundreds of Granitarians were in attendance. Many more outside the walls could hear the proceedings.

Alli caught herself staring. Soaking in their faces so she would never forget. She was communing with a completely unknown section of the human race. As the Granitarians rose to speak, she felt honored.

"Is it true? Did he steal from us?" A woman sitting in the lower half of the gallery directed her question toward Allis' guide. It was obvious she was angry. All eyes were on the guide. On Alli as well. She wondered if he was some kind of leader. Though there were no signs of him being treated with any special regard. They had been seated toward the front of the gallery. When he stood to answer, the gallery grew quiet. He leaned over and said, "Be patient Allison. Today is a turning point for our city."

"Yes, it is true. He's killing on the surface. There's much at stake." Another woman stood in the gallery. She was obviously frightened.

"I'm concerned we will be found out accidentally. Our children must be our main concern. We must evacuate them if necessary."

"The surface has never found us out! I believe with Allison Chapmans help we will resolve this problem and that will be the end of it. Also, I have talked to the extra-terrestrials. As far as they are concerned we are free to do what is necessary."

"Extra-terrestrials?" That was a new concept for Alli. She saw the ships parked at the Granitarian airport, but had not considered the implications.

"There's obviously a lot I have to learn." Her guide smiled and wrapped an arm around her.

"There's a few thousand years of things to learn, Allison." He turned back to the gallery.

"The immediate goal should be to stop the surface carnage. Allison must be allowed to help." The guide paused for a moment. There were whispers throughout the gallery. Alli could almost hear every conversation. The cavern did this. Even the slightest noise was amplified. She had seen this before. Sound can be very deceiving in caves.

What she was witnessing reminded her of the floor of the Senate when a vote was taking place. The people of Granitaria were trying to solve a problem and remain calm. Finally, someone way in the back stood and said, "Allison, one of your kind is to blame!"

At first she didn't understand. "Blame? Blame for what? I thought this had to do with your people."

"No Allison. The murderer is one of yours." Alli was caught off guard. She thought she was there to help catch one of their own. She had all but given up on the idea that it was someone from her world.

"This is bad!" She yelled. "Someone else from the surface knows about Granitaria?" Her voice carried throughout the city. "What has happened?" She demanded.

"His name is Cutter!" The same unseen voice rang out. That information brought more nervous chatter. Also the voice sounded angry. Her guide leaned over and whispered. "This is good. The truth is coming out." He stood again.

"Yes, she needs to hear it all. What he's capable of and why he's doing it." At that point he had Alli stand. He escorted her to the center of the complex. It was a signal to everyone that a "story" would be told. Granitarians revered story telling. It went back to the beginning. After the daily meal. Sitting around the fire telling stories of their daily lives. Hunting for food. Protecting their young. It was their tradition. It was deep rooted. For Granitarians it was holy.

The gallery grew quiet. This story was being told for the first time. The audience would remain quiet until the story tellers finished. Anyone could join in as long as they walked to the middle of the floor. This exercise was somewhat ceremonial. The Granitarians knew of

Cutter, but this was the first time a stranger was part of the public story telling. Alli's guide was the first to speak.

"Simply put, Allison, he's insane. He's become powerful because he carries some of our technology. Our ability to travel the stars has brought us great knowledge. We discovered a race of aliens. Or more accurately they discovered us. They've been coming here for a long time. They know we live under the surface. They don't understand why we don't rule over your people. You're less advanced. That's how their society works. We don't agree with that thinking. We are happy to share the Earth with you. We are all equal parts of this planet. But your world is not ready for ours."

It was expected that Alli should speak as well. She got that. But was not sure how to respond. She was still processing. Standing next to her guide, all eyes were on her. The cavern became overwhelming. The entire experience was almost too much. And now silence. All those people in total silence. She was experiencing true cave life. Not total darkness, but total silence. No cars. No airplanes. No voices. Just total silence. For a moment she thought she heard her own heartbeat. Seconds ticked by. Finally, her guide called her name.

"Allison. Are you all right?"

"Yes. Yes I am." She said. "I've seen the results of your technology. Does it give the killer an ability to travel with ease?" A beautiful woman stood a few rows up from the floor.

"Yes Allison. The user only needs to start the process. Then he may Particle Bore and begin again." Alli thought she saw the woman float as she came down the stairs. When she reached Alli, she moved close. Staring straight into her eyes.

"Allison, the horror of this weapon, is that everyone is a victim. The user. The used, and the dead. Certain individuals have the correct DNA to become killers. They gain the ability to float above the ground. A type of controlled flight. Then they simply touch their victims and they die. The killer doesn't remember what it has done. They become the perfect spy. Controlled by a single user."

Alli felt dizzy. Slightly nauseous. But under control.

"Their cells blow up and their heads turn around. I've seen it. How terrible." Her guide touched her on the shoulder.

"How the body looks after, is just a side effect."

The Granitarian woman made her way to the center of the floor. She sensed Alli was uncomfortable.

"Relax Allison. Your going to be all right. I think it would be wise if you were to sit in the gallery." Propping Alli up by one arm, her guide escorted her to an open seat at the edge of the floor. The woman remained to finish the story.

"Cutter wants to rule the world. We don't believe in that. He's stolen our technology and is using it to kill indiscriminately. The device is our atomic bomb. We developed it. We wish we hadn't. It's the price of our intelligence."

It was all making sense now. Alli had been allowed to come to Granitaria because the murderer was one of the six-billion suspects on the surface. No problem.

"How did he find this place? You have concealed yourselves all this time." Her question was a tipping point for the Granitarians. Continuing the story could lead to disclosing long kept secrets.

"Cutter told us he was an explorer. While caving in France he stumbled and started a cave in. In turn, he opened a new passage leading down to our caves. He was found in a side chamber miles from our main city, but still in our realm. He was close to death from exhaustion. We nursed him back to health and he stayed with us for a year. We allowed him to stay because we didn't want to be discovered. It was a mistake!"

Another woman joined them on the floor. She to floated from the gallery. Alli felt something negative from this woman.

"After he left, we back tracked his steps and found four dead cave explorers. Obviously from his party. They had been dead for about a year. He is a liar and a thief! And now he's a mass murderer!" The woman turned away from Alli and raised her voice. "Cutter's desire became obsession as soon as he learned of the aliens. He broke into one of our labs and stole what he needed. Now he's on the surface. Killing the innocent!"

Alli Chapman was an intuitive agent. She could always sense when a suspect was going to loose it. Get mad, throw things, generally yell and scream. No matter how this woman seemed for the moment, she was pushing the edge. Alli felt her hatred. The type of despise someone might have for everyone on the surface. Especially our politicians or anyone in authority. Whoever this Cutter was, he had endangered an entire planet. The known and the unknown. Alli was sad that things had turned out this way. The gallery remained silent. Alli took it as an opportunity.

"I need to ask your permission on an important matter." She was careful how she approached her next request. "May I tell one other person? I'm going to need help to find this man."

The complex irrupt with anger. Allis' question began a flood of retorts. One woman began crying as she shouted to the gallery.

"No, please, no one else can know! We are going to be found out! If not now, then in the future. It will come out. It's human nature!" Another man stood and yelled that bringing Alli to their home would be the end of their way of life.

"Wait.... Wait! The guide raised his voice to quiet the crowd. It finally grew quiet. Alli broke protocol and started up the stairs of the complex. All eyes were on her. Some with contempt.

"Listen to me!" She pumped her fist in anger. The raised her hands over her head to dispel further outburst.

"Listen to me. I trust the man I wish to tell. His name is Detective Tim Renolds. He brought me into this case in the first place. He can be trusted."

There was a long pause in the complex. Again it was very silent. No one else commented. The story was over. The Granitarians stood and began to file out. The guide waved her down to the edge of the floor.

"Your terms are acceptable, Allison. Now, I'll take you home."

"So that's it? I can tell my friend? No more discussion? They trust me?"

"Yes Allison. We trust you." In the next second Alli was home. Standing in her living room. She looked at the guide and said,

"Unbelievable." Her house was her home, but felt like a foreign country. There was some jet lag associated with traveling through miles of rock. She went outside and took some deep breaths. The sunlight was hard on her eyes. Her guide followed her. He to had to shield his eyes.

"These will protect you." He handed her two small oval devices. "They will protect you and we will be able to track you both.. Also, we have put together some of your currency. It's for any needs you have." Alli examined the cash. There was fifty-thousand dollars.

"If you need more, just wait. You will receive it." He took Alli's hand. She was unsure of the etiquette. Alli wanted to give him a hug, but did not.

"Allison Chapman, you've had a hard two days. You've been so brave. But please find this man and destroy him. Save us all. We cannot spend time on the surface. We could be stopped and questioned. That could lead to our city being found. It's too great a risk."

Alli studied the pale man. It was hard to believe what had taken place. She had so many questions, but one stood out. One question that would prove absolute trust between these two souls from different worlds. "Is Granitaria beneath France?"

"Yes Allison. You heard that did you? We are trusting you with our lives. Some secrets do not matter. Compared to what Cutter is doing to your people."

"Is there anything else you can tell me that might help locate him?" The gentleman thought for a moment.

"He once told me that he worked for an airline in Dallas, Texas. I don't know if that helps."

"It's a start," she replied. "If I were doing this right, I'd interview every Granitarian that had contact with him. It would help the investigation, but we don't have time, do we?"

"Allison, we are out of time. We were out of time with his first kill. Believe me, we will help you. Fine out as much as you can. We will watch. At the appropriate times, we will appear."

Alli wished he would stay. If he would just stay and help look for the killer. Certainly with this technology he would know what to look for. Instead, she asked one final question. "Does Cutter have a first name?" Her guide laughed, but shook his head.

"No." "We only called him Cutter."

Chapter 13

Alli hit the bed. She fell asleep instantly. It was hard work learning there was an entire civilization right under our feet. That there was a fantastic hidden city under ground. That she was the keeper of the greatest secret in the history of man. It made her a little tired. When Alli awoke some hours later, she remembered her dreams had been wild. She was still in bed when the phone alerted her to reality.

"Hello." She was not sure she wanted to talk to anyone out of fear they would ask the wrong questions. She might blurt out everything. It was Tim, of course. He started right in on her. Giving her a hard time.

"You got a boyfriend or something? You sure have been gone a lot. I called. I even came over." Her reply was short.

"No. But I need to see you."

"That sounds serious."

"It is. There's something I need to tell you. But it has to stay between you and me."

"Ok, I'm coming over." Tim was quick about it. He could tell there had been a break in the case or something was terribly wrong. When he arrived, Alli had coffee on and was sitting at her kitchen table.

"What's going on? Are you ok? I tried calling. You haven't been home. What's going on?" Alli sat quietly staring at the table. When she looked up at Tim, it was time to decide. Could he be trusted? She wanted to believe there was something between them. Something genuine. Something pure. From this point out. It was all about truth.

"What if I tell him everything and he runs to his boss?" She had to make the choice right then and there. "Tim wouldn't do that!" She thought. "I have to trust him."

"Tim, what I'm about to tell you is unbelievable and fantastic. You've never heard anything like this before. I think we are on our own with this case. We may get some help, but not from our people.

At least not early on." She paused to collect her thoughts. Tim almost yelled with anticipation, but held his tongue.

"This must be, no matter how it turns out, our secret to the end." With that, the detective turned from caring friend to professional cop.

"What the hell is going on? What do you know, Alli? Why would I need to make you a promise?"

"You have to promise me, Tim. I'm very serious. You either get it, or you don't." For a few moments he stared into Alli's eyes. She just stared back.

"Ok Alli. I swear on my life." He saw what he was looking for. In her persona. He saw the truth.

She told him everything. From being transported to a world under the crust of the Earth, to seeing flocks of space ships of different shapes and sizes.

"Tim, there were ships with triangular shapes, round with lights on the underside. I didn't get up close, but it was amazing! Everything about UFO's is true. The only difference is, they live here!" She told him about the strange man coming to her house and everything that followed. Alli told him about Cutter. She told him about story telling. When she had finished she simply asked, "Are you in or are you out?"

By this time, Detective Tim Renolds' mouth hung wide open. Twice he laughed out loud, but he knew the murders had to be something like this. Something supernatural.

"Wow!" A word Tim used when dealing with the outrageous. "This just took place?" He asked. "You were just there?"

"Yes." She said softly.

"Alli! Wow! I get it. I understand. I won't tell anyone. I'm in! Thanks for trusting me."

"Your my partner, partner. I need you with me. I even asked permission so I could tell you. At first they didn't like it. But after I told them about you, they didn't ask another question. They just walked out. It was their way of agreeing with my terms."

"This is a big deal, Tim. Our lives have just changed forever. I wish you had been there. It was unbelievable." Tim took her hand and pulled her close. They had hugged before but not like this. Alli felt warm. Then she gently pulled away. She reached up and touched his chin. "By the way, aliens do exist!"

The ride home was hard for Tim Renolds. He kept hearing her words, "Aliens do exist." Over and over in his head.

That night Alli slept soundly. Some weight was off her shoulders. She needed peace. She had an extraordinary experience, but there was a lot of work to do. Some of the hardest would be the very next day. They would have to deal with their respective superiors. It would be tough. Tim knew his boss could see through any B.S. It bothered him until he fell asleep.

Chapter 14

The personal secretary for Assistant Director Phillips allowed Alli to wait in his office. She liked Alli and had, on occasion, shared after work cocktails with her. A.D. Phillips was the regional bureau chief for the southwest. He liked Allison as well. He felt she was a great asset to the F.B.I. Mostly because she took on the hard cases.

"Allison "Alli" Chapman. What can I do for you?" She turned toward the door just in time to see him walk in.

"Hello, Sir. It's good to see you." It was already decided. The story would be they had an anonymous source. They would have to return to Texas.

"Well, Sir, Detective Renolds and myself might need to go back to Texas. We've received some new information related to "The Phenomenon."

"What kind of information?" Agent!?" With that question, Alli had to merge fact with fiction.

"Sir, my partner went to London, you know that odd story about a floating girl. We don't know what to think of that. But he learned that there may be a reason to interview some folks at the Dallas airport. It's all preliminary. Mostly background, trying to find a name connected with this tragedy."

"Do you suspect the killer might be from Dallas?"

"Don't know about that, Sir. Tim's source was anonymous, but maintained that we need to interview employees at the Dallas/Fortworth Airport."

"Alli, go. You two were right. We have really screwed this investigation up. If you think you've got a lead, run with it."

"Thank you, Sir." And with that, Alli headed out. Lying bothered her a little, but it was necessary.

Tim on the other hand, was caught. His boss said he had never seen such a bad liar, but wished him good luck anyway. The Captain knew his boy. He had nothing but respect for Detective Tim Renolds.

Alli purchased their tickets and as soon as they reached Dallas, they went right to work.

First, straight to the human resource office. It was the fastest way to search through hundreds of airport employees.

"We are looking for a man with the last name of Cutter. Can you help us?" Alli pulled her badge out to move the conversation along. "We don't have a first name so if there's more than one Cutter in your data base, I'll take them all."

"Cutter, that doesn't ring a bell. Let me check the payroll software. NO, no Cutter, but he could be employed by an individual airline. Also, the airport employs sub-contractors. He could work for one of them." Alli and Tim could see this was going to be an impossible job. They thanked the human resource lady and decided to split up. It was the best way to get Cutter's first name.

Alli canvas the concourses checking bars, restaurants, janitorial, and anyone that looked like they could help. Tim opted for the baggage handlers. Each airline had to be checked individually. After three hours and no joy, Alli called Tim on he cell phone. She was hungry and frustrated with the lack of success.

"Hey. No luck?" She asked.

"No luck, partner."

"Damn Tim. Talk about needles in haystacks. I looked in the phone book. There are a hand full of Cutters, but I know none of them are our guy. Maybe we'll track a couple of them down later. Just to be sure."

"Let's just call them up." Tim said. "Tell them we're selling something."

Detective Tim was trying to lighten the moment.

"No. You know damn well that would alert him. He'd run for sure. We've got to get his first name. It could lead to photo I.D's, or military information. Tracking down locals is a last resort."

After a meal, they returned to their task. Tim thought a golf cart was a necessary piece of equipment. If they were to continue.

The next morning they met in the motel lobby for breakfast. The prior day's search produced nothing. No one had heard of an employ named Cutter.

"I've got a question for you, girl. What do we do with this guy when we find him?" Tim was on his second cup of coffee. This subject was not covered in earlier conversation.

"We may have to kill him. In fact, he should be assassinated. He will kill us in a second. He can be anywhere. He must think the Granitarians are looking for him. What he doesn't know, is that two detectives from the surface know about him too. He's paranoid. Psychopathic, and delusional. He's got stolen technology that must be returned. If the Granitarians could find Cutter without our help, they would have. He has the advantage of split second travel. We'll never catch him. We have to lure him to us. Identify, track, and restrain his abilities. Then we might have a chance."

Tim Renolds was amazed at her logic. Her skill of deduction. Also, she made it clear. This was a hunting expedition. Luring their pray in close. Make him bring the fight to them.

Tim stared down at a Dallas Morning Newspaper. The lead read, "The Phenomenon" responsible for Thirteen-Hundred Deaths. Latest in Europe."

"What's he doing, Alli. Circumventing the globe?" Alli shook her head.

"No. With Particle Boring, he can jump anywhere. He's killing at random."

Tim continued eating his breakfast. Then in the middle of his last bite of waffle, he stopped.

"What did you just say?" Alli thought for a moment, "Jump anywhere?" As if they were lovers for fifty years staring into each others eyes and in one voice they both said, "The Space Station!"

"Oh my God, Tim!" Then for several seconds there was silence between them. The world seemed to fall away. Then in a whisper Tim said, "The ISS, what a place to hide." Alli stood. As if to go somewhere. Then stopped and sat down. "What are we going to do?" She asked.

"Can he do that?" Tim asked.

"Yes Tim. His technology will take him there. He can beam into local space." Alli thought about her trip through solid rock to get to Granitaria. "He could go there and eliminate the crew."

Tim's eyes told Alli everything she needed to know. He was a big fan of the space program. As a little boy he dreamed of walking in space. This revelation, made him mad.

"Tim, there's nothing we can do about it. We'll go to Houston. We'll go to Mission Control. I promise. But we have to finish here."

"Ok, Alli. We finish here then we go." NASA was a flight and a rental car away. When they resumed the search of the airport, their determination had been strengthened. Finally, this business was a mission.

They used their badges to move through security. A federal I.D. was handy to have along.

"No, I don't know that name." Alli spoke to a man with a broom in Delta concourse. As she interviewed him, someone interrupted. "Excuse me, are you the one looking for someone named Cutter?"

A woman stood behind Alli, so she spun around to see a face with a voice. "Yes, do you know him?"

"No, I don't know him, but I think he worked for the baggage delivery company. Yes. The lost baggage service. But that was a long time ago. Years I think."

Alli hit the concourse running! She barley turned around to thank the woman for the information.

"Thank you! Thank you very much!" She scrambled for her cell phone. "Tim, we might have caught a break! Meet me at Deltas' baggage claim right now!"

Tim flew down a long walk way, then a short escalator ride.

"Alli, what's up?"

"Hang on." She leaned over the counter and flashed her badge.

"Excuse me, do you have any employees with the last name Cutter?" The young woman behind the counter stopped smiling.

"No, he doesn't work for us. He worked for the delivery company. He's a real jerk too." Alli laughed and bumped Tim with her shoulder.

"This young lady remembers the guy!" Tim put on a grin from ear to ear. "What's his name honey?"

"His name is Martin Cutter, and he's always screwing with the girls here. He's a great big liar too. He's always telling stories about caves and places he's gone to. Just trying to impress us."

"Caves? He talked to you about caves? How long ago?"

"I don't know. He hasn't been around for a long time. We just figured he got fired. Why are you cops looking for him? Who did he kill?" Alli laughed and gave her a big smile. "We just wanted to talk to him. You know, just a person of interest." Alli slid by the girls' question, but they both knew the answer. If Martin Cutter was "The Phenomenon" he had killed a lot of people. Alli thanked the girl and grabbed Tim's arm.

"We found him! His name is Martin Cutter! I'm sure it's him. Telling these gals stories about caving. No way it's not him."

Leaving the airport, there were high-fives all around. When they returned to the motel, they went straight to the lounge. It was late. The detectives chose to stay another night before heading to Houston.

Tim convinced Alli to join him for a dance. The music was mellow and though she protested, Alli enjoyed the evening. In the middle of the second song, she pulled back. "I've got to get some sleep. You should too." She gave Tim a hug, turned and walked out. On the way back to her room, she disciplined herself.

"He's your partner, damn it! Stay focused. There's still a lot to do." She could have spent the night criticizing behavior unbecoming. But Alli loved dancing. Dancing with Tim. She adored him. He made her so happy. She screamed into her pillow.

That night she dreamed. First of flying through space. Then running through a tunnel as it fell in on her. That got her up for a while. It felt real. Real enough she grabbed at her own arm when she came around. She went back to sleep. One more dream, that night. Back in the same tunnel. This time she was not alone.

Tim stayed for one more drink. They had had some success. It made the whole story all the more real. Yesterday they chased bad guys with guns. Now, they were chasing a ghost. A killer that could come and go as he pleased. Bore through rock. Bend Space- Time. Or, whatever?

"I'm working for people I can't talk about." He whispered. A woman sitting two seats down looked over at him. She frowned when she saw he was sitting alone.

"What if we can't find him?" Tim turned his head. Not much. Just enough to let his neighbor know he had caught the frown. Then, repeated his question. A little louder.

"What if we can't find him and he goes on killing?" She took a drink. Sat her glass down and left.

"What then?" He said.

The moment Alli went to her room, he missed her. Then there was Alli.

Chapter 15

In the morning, Tim expressed his disdain for early rising. Though he was happy their airport Easter egg hunt was over. When he saw Alli in the hall, he called out.

"Are we going to Houston?" A simple question. One he felt he needed to remind her of.

"Not yet." She snapped. I'm calling the baggage delivery company. I want to talk to Cutter's ex-boss. Call me OCD, but profile is my middle name." She reached the company's owner. Cutter had worked there. The owner relayed that Cutter had washed out of the Army when he failed the Psychological exam. That he was excepted at first. But his commander started seeing strange behavior. When he was reevaluated by the doctors, it was clear he would not or could not take orders. It was little things. Like pulling the trigger when he was told to stop. That might have had something to do with it.

"So, he was military?" Tim Renolds was in the first Gulf war. He took notice of any bad guy that had military training.

"Time to watch your back, partner." He said. Alli smiled a long smile. Then reciprocated.

"Thanks for your concern." Then she glared at him. A glare that said, "Pull your head out." Before he could respond, she said "Let's go to Houston."

Investigating NASA should be a big deal. Normal procedure would be to contact Alli's boss. A.D. Phillips. He would contact someone in Washington. Permission would be given. Possibly a warrant would be issued. The FBI in D.C. would contact NASA. Appointments would be made. etc., etc. There was no time for all that. No time for kid gloves. Bad things were happening. But Alli and her detective were acting on a hunch. There was no proof of any wrong doing at the I.S.S. NASA is a serious place. With serious people running it. The type of people that ask questions for a living. There could be nothing said out of the ordinary. It had to remain a simple interview. The hard part would be explaining why they were there in the first place.

"When we get to Houston, let's keep it routine." She said. Alli was a bit concerned. Tim might pin someone against a wall to get the truth.

"Just ask about the mission status. Anything that keeps the conversation light until we know what's going on. No mention of mass murder. Ok?"

"I know, Alli. If we say the wrong thing, it could lead back to Granitaria." He was still upset with the possibility of a murdered crew. However, this time Alli would do all the talking.

Chapter 16

Deep in the North Atlantic Ocean, one of Granitarias circular craft quietly exits a large cave. Many such caves are part of a vast network in the Graitarian realm. It was believed that a ship should be available. Allison and her partner could need help. What type of assistance, and the extent there of, became points of Granitarian debate.

Some crew members wanted nothing to do with the surface. They would just as soon reverse course. Surface humans were dangerous. Granitarians had their own word for humanity. No. For them, this was dangerous. Even though their technology could shield them. Their hearts were human. Thus, a certain amount of jealousy existed. Discovery is the greatest fear. The single most important reason for their lives. Fifteen millenia had past. They weren't scared of loosing their way of life. They were scared of war with the surface. If they were found out, there would be no choice. Jealousy would take over. These are special conditions. The operation had to go on.

Chapter 17

The flight from Dallas took 42 minutes. The plan was to land in Houston, rent a car, and show up at Mission Control. No badges necessary. They were just tourists. Sort of.

"Seems to me we shouldn't have any problem talking to someone in charge. Isn't NASA kind of slow these days? They only have the ISS to worry about. We should get right in." Tim realized his nervous talk gave him away. It was the space station. He was really worried.

"Let's hope everything is ok, Tim. I'd hate to see anyone up there get hurt. It makes me sick to think about all the innocent people this guy is destroying. But if we can think of this, so can he."

Tim did not say much after that. Alli's thoughts agitated him. He was never much of an emotional type, but he envisioned his first trip to NASA a bit differently. As they approached the front gate, it was obvious something had happened.

Security was everywhere. Automatic weapons were out. It looked as if the mundane and routine had been replaced with mayhem. Maybe badges would work, maybe they wouldn't.

"Stop right there!" The gate cop was surrounded by five or six well armed back-up.

"I'm detective Tim Renolds from the Phoenix Police department, and this is FBI Chapman. We're on official business and would like to talk to whomever is in charge."

"This ain't a good time!" The guard was convincing.

"What has happened?" Alli leaned over to address the guard.

"Don't know ma'am. The brass just sounded the alert."

"Sergeant, we need to talk to the flight control people. It's a matter of national security, and life and death. Do you get what I'm saying?" The guard got on the phone and twenty seconds later opened the gate.

"Thank you Sergeant." Tim saluted on the way in. "Oh, who do we see?" The guard pointed to a lead car with a flashing light on top.

"This car will guide ya'all to Mission Control. Follow it! Don't do anything else. You will be met."

They followed the car to Mission headquarters and remained in their vehicle as they were told. After a couple minutes, a man in a suit approached them and said, "Come with me."

They got out and followed him. As they walked, he introduced himself as Director Steve Bennett. Director Bennett was a serious man and all he wanted to know was what the hell they were doing there? Alli Chapman was an extremely pleasant individual, but at times she felt there were no choices in a given situation. Straight forwardness, no matter the cost was the plan B! So before Tim could stop her, or cover her mouth, she said, "Mister Bennett, are your people in the Space Station ok?"

"Oh, crap! How did you know?" The party came to an abrupt halt in the middle of the corridor. "No. We haven't heard from them for hours."

"I kind of thought so, sir. When we pulled up and saw all the guns, it screamed of something being screwed up and no one knows how to fix it!" Alli was a natural smart-ass! Bennett didn't care for the comment, but he got it.

"We can't contact them. I'm afraid there's been a catastrophic failure. It looks as though the station is intact. But no response and no SOS. But with you two here, I'm guessing there's a lot more." There was a long pause at which time Tim considered picking Alli up and running for the door. But he was too late.

"They're probably dead, sir. Murdered!"

Tim stared wide eyed at Alli! He couldn't believe what she was saying. She hadn't wasted any time.

"Murdered, what the hell are you talking about?" The flight director did not like where this was going. Alli filled him in. Only to the part that it could be related to "The Phenomenon" killings. And that the individual they were looking for could be hiding on the Space Station.

"That's insane!" Bennett was furious. "What kind of people are you?" Alli struck back with tenacity.

"We know what we're talking about, sir. We are the original detectives on "The Phenomenon" case. We can't go into why we suspect this, but it's possible someone has figured out a way to get to the station. Without you knowing about it."

In the same breath, Alli settled things down by asking Director Bennett for an office. She and Tim needed to contact their superiors.

"Ya! I'd like to talk to them as well! But I'm too damn busy right now!" He pointed to an office with a phone. Tim followed Alli into the office and shut the door.

"What are you doing? You really caught me off guard." Tim said.

"I changed my mind." She said sternly.

"I get that. But you damn near told him the whole story. What if he starts an investigation?" Alli got face to face with the detective.

"This guy Bennett is a problem. I'm not waiting for him to come around. Besides, he doesn't believe me. The I.S.S. is compromised. You know it, Tim. That's what all this is about. Bennett's busy with that. He won't tell anybody. He'll stay the course, and run the NASA playbook. Until another solution is discovered."

Alli turned away from her partner. For a moment neither detective said a word. When she turned back, she remembered Tim's admiration for the space agency.

"I'm sorry about the I.S.S." She said. "Unfortunately, our guesses have been pretty good. We have to lure him to us. We have to do it soon. Cutter is obviously feeling safe. We don't want that. We can't contact the Granitarians, but hopefully they're tracking us and have figured out what we know."

Thousands of years of technology. Of course they were tracking them.

The space station was silent. The storage area. The labs and medical. The exercise equipment. All silent. The only sound was communications repeating, "This is Mission control. Please respond, over." The station was silent except for the sounds of a maniac planning his war on humanity. What better way to anger a couple of nations, than to bring down their space station. Hundreds of strange murders all over the world. Then a high emotion event like an explosion in space to push people over the edge. Make them nervous. Make them hate like he did. Begin the war. When it was done, keep only what served him. Gold. Women. Just set the explosives. The I.S.S. would re-enter the Earth's atmosphere for maximum effect. If it landed on a city, all the better.

Maybe they killed themselves. Maybe each other. Tim Renolds kept picturing it in his mind. It would forever haunt him. Many years would pass before he would drink enough to mourn. Alli had never seen him cry. The anguish he displayed that night, made her weep as well. Tim wanted to be an astronaut. But she was his favorite hero. Favorite. Best. Most. He drank a lot that night.

Cutter had murdered the crew. Ejected the bodies into space. Planted his bombs and never thought twice. This was his new head quarters. It would serve two purposes. Safe haven. Where no one could reach him. When the time was right, a weapon. Proof he was humanities master.

The stolen technology gave him power. Power for his revenge. On a society that called him a fool. A word he knew well. Unfortunately, society missed this fool's potential. Someone once said,

"When you see something, say something." The girl at the airport that remembered his name, never said a word to the authorities. She knew Martin Cutter was a creep, but must have thought him harmless. Or he went away. She didn't have to think about him any more.

When Cutter stumbled on to Granitaria, he found the gold he'd been searching for. One small device that had but one purpose. Ultimate power.

Chapter 18

Upon their return to Phoenix, an odd meeting took place. As the detectives exited the concourse at Sky Harbor Airport, they saw a woman holding a poster board with their names on it. When they approached her, she identified herself as a partner in a local law firm. She had been retained by an unknown client to deliver two envelopes. One for each of them. Marked confidential both notes read,

"Extremely important to be at FBI agent Allison Chapmans' home by seven PM." A second piece of paper had a large symbol in the middle. A perfect triangle with a candle in the center.

The first note was easy enough. But the symbol made no sense.

"What the hell is this?" Tim asked.

"I don't know." Alli turned to the lawyer.

"What's this all about? Who is your client?"

"I don't know, miss. Someone walked into our office and left this with my secretary. Along with a healthy retainer."

"You don't know this symbol?" Tim asked.

"No. My instructions were only to deliver. It's not unusual for lawyers to do such things. The retainer was obviously to make sure it got done."

"Ok." Alli said. "We'll take it from here." As the lawyer walked away, Tim winked at Alli.

"This is from our Granitarian buddies, isn't it?"

"Of course it is. Don't be late, Tim. Be on time. They will. They must have important news. But as far as this symbol, your guess is as good as mine."

"I'll be at your place at seven." Tim was excited. For him, meeting the Granitarians was better than the President. Way better.

When he arrived at Allis home, he found her staring at her protection device.

"I wonder how this technology works? The Granitarians are thousands of years a head of us. How could that have happened if we all started out the same?" Tim removed his device from his pocket.

"I don't let this out of my sight. It's the only counter measure we have to combat Cutter. His device and ours must us microscopic electronics. I think our engineers are there, but I'm sure we don't have anything this powerful." Alli held her device up for inspection.

"These might save our lives some day."

A moment later and in a flash of light, the detectives were standing on the bridge of a flying saucer! Tim Renolds looked around at the crew. Their pale complexion and the soothing light throughout the ship. It made him say, "Wow!"

"Hello Allison, nice to see you again." Her guide from Granitaria stood before her.

"This is my partner, Detective Tim Renolds."

"Hello, Detective, welcome."

"Wow!" Tim's vocabulary had not changed much.

"Yes Allison, you found Cutter's hide out; but he's all ready left. The crew is dead. You know that, don't you?"

"Yes. They suspected it on the surface as well." It made Alli sad to talk about it. "They can't contact the space station and that's put my government on high alert."

"That is all right, Allison. It's better this way. With your government nervous and busy, we can plan the unfortunate destruction of your space station." The cave dweller and his crew could not reach the station in time to save the astronauts.

"So, you guessed?" Alli asked.

"Only where you two lead us. It was your investigation that gave us the obvious. We just had to watch you. Even we didn't think of your space station until you went to NASA."

"You are tracking us?"

"Yes. Your protection devices are specifically designed for that task. Monitor you and your partner, and protect you both."

"How do they work? What is their range? Is it two way? Can we contact you?"

"No! No, Allison. All you need to know is that the devices protect you and serve us." That was the first time Alli heard the Granitarian exert a negative. So much for diplomacy.

"Allison, we think Cutter is working in Peru. We think he's stock piling weapons for some kind of war." Her guide went on to explain that Cutter learned about the cave from the Granitarians. "It's well hidden. Surface people haven't even seen the entrance in four hundred years. Embedded in the walls of this cavern, are beautiful jewels, long forgotten by the native people. Modern surface dwellers have been gently made unwelcome whenever they stumble on it's location. Sometimes they even see a ghost!"

A woman Alli remembered from the open air complex stepped forward and spoke in her soft direct tone.

"When Cutter found out about the cave, he wouldn't stop talking about it. He was obsessed! He is selfish and vain. We refused to take him there. This action could be one of the catalyst that drove Cutter away. We're sorry we didn't think to tell you this sooner, but it has come to our attention that weapons have been stolen from two of your army bases. We are sure it's him." Alli thought about it and decided to test their arrangement.

"So, the reason you called us here is two fold? You have this lead for us, Peru? Are you admitting, Cutter knows more of your secrets? Is there anything more dangerous than the device he has stolen? Is there anything you've left out? Something more we should know so we can protect ourselves?" There was silence from the Granitarians. Whether they were surprised at Allis' tone, or they simply did not want to answer, Alli could not tell. It made her feel a little uneasy, but not enough to send her packing. Though Tim noticed her intent. The situation called for a bit of detached empathy. Alli backed off. The slender Granitarian woman ignored Allis' queries. It was expected that a surface dweller with Allis' intelligence would ask such questions. The woman continued.

"The weapons are in a vertical cave, not far from the Nazca Lines."

"Why am I not surprised?" Alli said under her breath. She loved this stuff! And she loved caves! She wanted to ask about the Nazca Lines and if they had anything to do with them. She suspected they did, but held her tongue.

"We wish to beam you there now."

"To Peru?" That caught Alli off guard. Her thoughts ranged from alerting her boss that she wasn't coming to work, to she wasn't dressed for the terrain. "Oh well," she thought. "I'll change down there."

"Chase him down, Allison. Do whatever is necessary. If you don't kill him, push him out of his comfort zone. Take the cave and it's contents. If Cutter returns to the Space Station, we will be ready."

Detective Tim had been admiring everything in the saucer. He finally made it into space! He took note of all the controls and hundreds of small lights floating out away from the control panels. It seemed for every light on the panels, a corresponding light hovered one or two feet away. Like a hologram, but different.

"Controls made convenient?" He wondered. The deck of the saucer was completely open. All the controls and seating were around the circumference. Tim thought it looked comfortable. He smiled and shook the hand of every cave dweller he came to. However, he kept an ear on the discussion. This was Allis' show. But when he felt the time was right he asked.

"You Granitarians are going to help us get this guy, right?"

"Yes Detective. Go with Allison to Peru. She needs you. You need each other." Tim smiled at the pale man. Though he thought the statement curious. "She needs you?"

Alli took Tims' hand. They were on an incredible adventure. They gazed out a long thin window. The view was beyond words. Earth was far below. The saucer was programmed to move in synchronous orbit with South America. They felt humble, and closer to one another. Tim squeezed Alli and whispered in her ear. She turned and faced the cave dweller.

"Before we go, may I ask what the symbol on your invitations represents? We don't understand." The Granitarians standing on the bridge made eye contact with one another. It was obvious to the duo that they were communicating with each other. It was as if they were deciding what to say. Finally her guide spoke.

"This is complicated, Allison. This symbol is from your people. Possibly from your government. The "Candle in the Triangle" is an action started by humans on the surface. We have physically felt it in Granitaria for some time now. We don't completely understand, but this symbol is connected some how. We've been monitoring surface computer conversations. It is within our capability."

"You can feel things happening on the surface?" Alli asked.

"Never before have we felt any man made disturbance such as this. It has to be massive!"

"Is this connected to Cutter? Is he doing something?"

"No. Watch for this symbol. It has nothing to do with Cutter directly, but we fear the killings on the surface may be exploited politically. Even after you capture Cutter, be aware. You obviously did not know of this. We are showing it to you as a warning. It does not effect us. It is for you."

The Granitarians explanation of the "Candle in the Triangle" was interesting, but that was all. It left the detectives confused. Something they didn't need right now. Neither Alli, nor Tim had ever heard of a business or corporation that used that standard.

Alli had a thousand questions, but they had a job to do.

"Farewell, FBI agent. Watch over her detective. We will be watching as well."

Chapter 19

In a flash. Two detectives beamed from orbit. The saucer set them down in a secure location not far from Lima. They had to walk a while, but no one witnessed their arrival. Particle Boring was truly amazing.

The first rule of cave exploration was preparedness. They would need a truck, appropriate cloths, food, water, and the best climbing gear they could find in Lima. Equipment such as ropes, pitons, and helmets. Preferably with built in lanterns. It saved on manhandling flashlights. These were the bare essentials. All the supplies had to be purchased without drawing much attention. They didn't need curiosity seekers following them to their destination. Without fail, there was always the character that noticed the two Americans purchasing equipment in search of buried treasure. That would just lead to someone getting killed. Surprisingly, they were able to acquire all they needed without any trouble. The duo spent the evening resting and started out for Nazca in the morning.

The plan was to drive south to the Nazca plain then turn inland to the cavern location. It was a long drive. Tim drove the first leg. Alli went through some verbal instruction on how to use climbing gear. Tim listened intently, but when she gave him the safety speech he spoke up.

"I'm not tying the knots! That's your job. I'd be afraid I was tying a slip knot. Down I'd go!" Alli laughed and reassured him. She was glad he was her partner in all of this.

"I'm sorry we aren't flying over the geoglyphs." She explained further. "A plane can't go where we are going. Maybe some day we will come back. When this is all over." With one hand on the steering wheel, Tim reached for her shoulder. He squeezed, then placed her hand in his.

"I'm going to tell you something girl. You're amazing and beautiful. There! I said it. I hope we do a lot of things when this is all over." Alli stared forward and smiled. They had a long way to go.

The trip was long and dusty. They took turns driving and kept the conversation professional. This was a mission. They were searching for Martin Cutter. A serial killer and enemy of two worlds. It had to have their best effort.

Alli drove while Tim slept. Occasionally looking over at him. With the windows cracked, dust crept in and caked their faces. Tim had a fake tan. She turned the mirror away. No need for torture. It looked good on him.

She thought about the FBI. It was her life. She was just one of the boys. After all, it was the FBI. There were a lot of boys. Alli even teased.

"Somebody sexually harass me so I can file a law suit!" Her coworkers loved her. She had their respect. When she was young, there were a couple boy friends, but the bureau took their place. She loved the job. And the adventure. However, this man affected her in ways she was unfamiliar with. He was in her life. Constantly, continually. Their professional relationship might not change for years. He was her best friend. He treated her with warmth.

The road hypnotized her. She knew she would surrender to him.

When they reached their destination they were able to park close to the cave entrance. The area was over grown with vegetation and surrounded by rolling hills. An airplane would have never been able to get in close. Getting the truck was the right call. Alli hopped out of the truck, shotgun in hand. Cutter could be anywhere. Tim pulled out the map and laid it on the hood of the truck.

"I'm looking at the name of the province we are in. It has so many X's and O's in it, it must be computer code. Not a name!" Alli told him to shut up and keep quiet, but she thought he was funny. As they surveyed the area there was no sign of Cutter. No tracks or disturbed plant life.

Alli walked Tim to the edge of the opening and peered down.

"I don't know Alli, I've never done this." Tim wished he could stay on top and not lower himself into the great hole.

"It's all right, I'll do all of the heavy lifting. You just have to ride it out." Allis' experience was reassuring, but he figured it was like military training. His C.O. almost had to push him out during flight school. However, this was serious business. Although it appeared that no one had been outside the cave, Cutter could have easily beamed deep inside. Concealing any sign of his presence.

While the duo removed the climbing gear from the truck, an important topic was revisited. If Cutter was in the cave, how was he to be treated?

"So Alli, if we run across this guy down there, do we shoot to kill?" This was her territory. Tim was just reaffirming her position. She had made it clear in Dallas. He had no problem with it.

"Tim, he'll kill anyone that gets in his way. We can't act like cops. We're assassins. He's an insane mass murderer. We can't allow him to escape."

Attaching ropes to a sturdy tree and safety lines to the truck bumper, the pair harnessed up and began the decent. The opening was large enough for both to go together, but Alli went first. Backing into the great hole. Showing Tim how it was done. Three to four feet of ledge, then dropping into open space. Hanging by two lines, she whispered, "See, it's easy. Now walk it down. Let the rope slip a little to reach me." Tim got the hang of it quickly. Some of his previous training kicked in. Immediately they realized the cave was not that deep. There was a ledge about fifty feet down. From now on they would use hand signals. No more talking. Sound travels in a cavern. Down they went. When they reached the ledge, they rested. And weapons came out. Alli went the next twenty-five feet to the cave floor in one leap. Tim thought to himself, "She's done this before." He followed, but she had already disconnected her lines and was checking out the immediate area of the cave. Her shotgun at the ready. Alli placed a finger over her mouth. She was listening for Cutter. In caverns there are always noises. Falling rocks, mice, insects, bats. This cave was too quiet. Tims' sidearm was out now. A chill raised the hair on the back of his neck. The cave gave him the creeps! Halogen lamps flickered on as they stumbled over medium sized rocks that lined the cave floor. The floor slanted downward in one direction. It seemed to be the way they should go. About one-hundred feet down, they came to a divide. A split in the path. With two different passages to choose from. Tim signaled. "Stay together or split up." Alli shook her head. Stay together it was. Down what looked like a more worn path, they chose to go right. The path got easier, but the ceiling was growing closer. Eight feet down to six. Trying to walk quietly and duck at the same time was a task.

Alli listened for the slightest noise. Tim spun around several times, watching the rear. Suddenly, about twenty yards in front of them, was a light. A slight stream of light. It was hard to tell if it was natural or synthetic. Guns were up. As well as the creep factor. But when they reached the end of the tunnel, it opened into a great room. They found the light was natural. Sunlight was streaming through a space almost one- hundred feet up. There was a crack in the crust!

They didn't know it at the time, but the Moche Indians called the room, "Gods' Doorway." They were fabulous pottery and jewelry makers. Some of the best ever known. The detectives would soon see. The Moche loved this cave.

As they entered, they were engulfed by thousands of sparkling points of light! Sunlight lit up the walls. Gems! Mostly quartz. But there were diamonds as well.

"No one knows about this place?" Tim whispered, then pointed to an area in the corner. "Guns Alli."

"Ya, I see them." The sunlight was lighting up a weapons cash as well. Automatics, hand held rocket launchers, and grenades. Lots of firepower. Cutter had been there. "War it's going to be." Alli thought. She turned to her left to touch the wall and there in front of her was Cutter! He was floating! Off the ground about four feet. Laid out flat so he could move through the cave. As he floated toward her, he let out a blood curdling scream! As if to say, "What the hell are you doing in my cave?" Alli fell over backwards and hit the floor hard. Tim reacted by going to her first. Instead of firing his weapon.

"Alli, are you all right?" He instinctively stepped in front of the FBI agent, shielding her from the attack.

"Go get him damn it!" Her demand echoed through the cavern. Her voice took over as Cutters' scream ended.

Tim and Alli stared at the floating man. He scared them both. She wanted to get up, but couldn't. She wanted to run, but she was paralyzed with fear. Funny things happen to the human body when you are frightened. Muscles tighten, and eyes close. Perception gets thrown out.

She was confused. Something odd was happening. And what was that smell? She could smell cookies. Cookies baking at her Grandmothers. And gravy! The white kind her Grandma made with fried chicken. What was going on?

Then she was back. Back in the cave. Her ears rang and the back of her head hurt. That was from the fall.

"Where are you, Tim? Are you all right?" What seemed like a long time, took a single moment. Tim was right there. Protecting her. He never left her side.

Cutter frantically pushed on something in his hand. The Device. He was trying to initiate the field. Forcing one detective to kill the other. It was the first time his device was not working. The field was allowing him to float, but not effect them at all. Cutter had never experience this. What was wrong?

Their protection devices were blocking the signal. The devices worked and protected them. Tim fired his weapon, but missed. The bullet ricochet off the cave wall. Forcing Cutter to retreat back down the passage. Tim looked back at Alli, and took out after him.

Alli was furious with herself.

"Get up! Get off your ass and fire your weapon." Much easier said than done. She had just witnessed Cutter's abilities for the first time. The vision of him floating was permanently etched in her head. A human being floating without any apparent means of doing so, can have a huge impact on even the most well trained FBI agent. She was still shaken, but yelled down the tunnel.

"Kill him Tim! Shoot the SOB." She pulled herself up. Rubbing the back of her head.

"Damn. What was I thinking? My partner's chasing the bad guy. I'm laying down on the job."

When she caught up with Tim, Cutter was no were in sight.

"Did you hit him" She asked.

"No. He just Particle Bored out of here. He was right in front of me, then he just disappeared. At that moment he left a faint point of light. Then it was gone. It was the most amazing thing I've ever seen."

"Tim. I'm sorry. I don't know what I was thinking."

"There was nothing we could have done. We saw the light and the guns, but we didn't clear the room. We got distracted. Besides. How do we fight that technology? Our protection devices worked, but he can just leave if he doesn't want to fight."

Alli stared straight ahead. She was embarrassed and angry.

"I'll never forget his face," she said. "I'll work the facial recognition software when we get home." For a moment Tim looked at her, then looked away. Not in anger. He was scared. Not of Cutter. He almost lost Alli.

"Let's get these guns dealt with and go home. I've had enough caving." He said.

Chapter 20

Alli and Tim caught the first flight out of Peru. Their itinerary had them stopping in Mexico City, then home to Phoenix.

Before they left, they contacted two FBI operatives and had them remove and store the stolen weapons. Alli knew the agents and asked for their discretion. They did as she asked. Forgetting any paperwork. Stolen military weapons might come in handy later on.

Unbeknownst to the passengers, the Granitarians followed their flight. If anyone on the flight had been able to look directly behind, they would have seen a bright saucer shaped craft. In fact, it flew directly behind and slightly below the tail of the jet. The pilots never saw a thing. Allis' pale companion was watching over them. He worried that Cutter might try something after the action in the cave. However, after they landed in Phoenix, the saucer instantaneously appeared back at the Space Station to search for Cutter. He had not returned.

During the flight, Alli tried to sleep but the image of Cutter floating kept her awake. At one point she gazed at Tim to start a conversation, but the look on his face stopped her. He was staring at the seat in front of him. Motionless and angry. They had faced Cutter and lived, but it was a missed oper-opportunity. It could never happen again! There were too many lives at stake. Too many had been lost.

"Alli, we didn't win this one."

"No Sir, we didn't." She responded.

"Girl, I think we're going to have to act like real cops. No more screwing around! We need to tell the world to be-on-the-lookout for Martin Cutter. Just like we would with a normal suspect."

Allison wanted to protest. A little, but did not. She wanted to remind Tim that they had an obligation to protect the Granitarian secret. That a world wide BOLO could lead to questions they might not be able to answer. However, now was not the time. Let Tim have his say.

"We start by telling our superiors that we screwed up! We admit we followed a lead without knowing all the facts, and should have called for backup. If we had come home with his head, none of this would be necessary. Now we don't have a choice."

Tim was right. If they had brought Cutter back, they would be heroes. Instead they had to ask for help. Alli chose not to press the subject. She knew damn well Tim would never give up the Granitarians, but she was still down about her conduct in the cave. Tim saved her life. He was the hero.

After several minutes of silence, Alli shifted in her seat. She wanted to face him.

"I only have one request." She tried not to grin as she completed the statement.

"Don't tell anybody in my office that we got abducted by a flying saucer, then beamed down to Peru. My co-workers would never let it go. I don't want them laughing at me."

Tim managed a smile, then let out a laugh.

"Damn, that's funny! I won't, Alli. If I did, they'd throw us in the loony bin." The levity lightened the mood. Tim was loosening up. Kicked his isle seat back. He was mad at himself. Not capturing Cutter. He wanted to do it for her.

The bureau had to be filled in. The press as well. Alli got a good look at Cutter. They both did. That was their ace in the hole. They could identify him. For the first time since the investigation started, the cops had something to go on. Before Peru, there was nothing. Cutter never left a trail. No photos or military I.D. Not even a phone number. He was meticulous. Erasing all permanent record of himself.

"Alli, we're not going to lie to our people. We'll tell them our investigation in Dallas lead us to Peru. That's it! We found him hiding in a cave, but he got away. We'll add that we should have called for help and let the cards fall were they may." Allison agreed. It was very possible they would be reprimanded.

When they arrived home, their superiors hailed the job in Peru a success! A major break in the case. Once the respective agencies circulated a composite drawing of Martin Cutter, a.k.a.

"The Phenomenon" killer, no hard questions had to be answered. FBI Chapman and Detective Renolds had put all law enforcement agencies closer to capturing the serial killer. Alli's boss paraded her in front of several Arizona politicians that were touring the Phoenix bureau.

While shaking hands with a Senator and pulling Alli into the photo op with an arm around her waste, her Section Chief repeated how proud he was of her tireless work. That the investigation would not have moved along without her. Though Alli smiled for the cameras, she was uncomfortable. Besides herself, only Tim knew what really happened in Peru. But now the world had a suspect! Martin Cutter. Finally, authorities had a place to start.

An international manhunt began. Fueled by the press doing exactly what it had done for decades. What it was ordered to do. Cutters' image was on front pages around the world. Billboards with slogans that read "This is the face of The Phenomenon Killer" were strategically placed on highways and the sides of buildings. It was encouraged that children learn to identify Cutter by sight. They were to report to their parents or someone in authority. From the start, reported sightings overwhelmed the police. None panned out. They tried to keep up, eventually only following the most promising leads. Meanwhile the murders continued. The press covered it all. Good or bad. The networks were fed talking points on a regular schedule. They did their job following orders. Reporting exactly what Alli and Tim wanted. They wrote the script and their superiors released it without question.

Tim always knew the press was on the take, but this was solid evidence. For him, this proved the symbiotic relationship between the Government and the press. The most powerful institutions conspire to control the flow of information to Fly-Over country. Miss lead and keep those tax dollars coming in. Keep those folks in their place. The detectives were government issue, too. But their message was that Martin Cutter was armed and dangerous. He was a coward that hid in the shadows and killed three at a time. By the time the press got done he was a monster that stole children for unspeakable crimes.

Chapter 21

Sitting at her desk, Alli's thoughts were of Granitaria. She rarely thought about anything else. It had been days since her last contact with the people underground, and there had been no movement in the case. Only more death.

Tim was busy with paper work, but they talked on the phone. "Don't worry Alli, you'll hear from them soon enough. They're probably watching the I.S.S. Cutter might return there."

"I know, but I'm more comfortable when they're around. I'm just stir crazy!"

"Your a warrior! You need action. Not what I'm doing. Back logged paper work. It sucks!"

Just then Alli received a memo at her desk.

"I just got word. There's been six more killings. Three in Russia and three more in the U.S. He's not sitting around. The jerk! What are we going to do about it?"

"Alli, our plan has to be done in stages. You know that. Phase one has been put into place. Tell the world what he looks like and make him mad at us. Make Cutter uncomfortable. Make him nervous. Right now we have to wait. We can't stop what he's doing. It's unfortunate, but we can't fight him now. He's going to do what he's going to do."

"I appreciate your thoughts. It's just that this case is different. They want us to save the world."

"Ya, they do." Tim said. Alli's frustration began to dissipate. Though "The Phenomenon" case was the big one, there were other fish to fry. Cutter was not the only killer out there. Alli hung up the phone and picked up another case file. A man had killed his family in Kingman, Arizona, and promptly disappeared. Local and state police were searching for him, but they felt an FBI profiler should be called in. Alli contacted them and requested more information be emailed to her. If she could, she would head up to Kingman at the end of the week. She was working a very important case, but she would see what she could do.

That evening, Tim drove by Alli's home. The lights were on so he decided to make his presence known. Tim knocked on the door and she answered.

"Hey Tim." She was surprised to see him. "Is something wrong? Is it Cutter?"

"No, I was just checking on you. Just driving by."

"It's not too late. Come in and I'll make you coffee. Or something stronger if you like."

"No, but I'll come in for coffee."

The pair sat at Allis' now familiar kitchen table. At first, Tim sat quietly, waiting for her to start a conversation. She did.

"So, you were just out driving and thought you'd better come see if Cutter was floating around my house!" Tim coughed and cleared his throat.

"I'm just watching your back. Would it feel better if I said I just wanted to see you?"

"I know Tim, and yes. It would feel better." She poured the coffee and sat two cups on the table.

"I've had enough of this guy. We've got to get him!" She said. Tim stared at her for a moment, then took her hand.

"You know, sitting on our butts is part of what we do as cops. I've spent a lot of time on stake outs and that is, without a doubt, the most boring job there is. Unfortunately, I wouldn't have made detective without it. Do stake outs pay off? Not very often, but you get to know the players. Sometimes that's enough."

She was happy he came by. Tim was a calming influence. She had done a little butt sitting her self, but obviously Tim was the expert. Local law enforcement worked very hard. Busting drug dealers sometimes took hours of surveillance. There was a lot of butt sitting needed. Made for great overtime pay.

"You're the best partner I've ever had." She gripped Tim's hand a little tighter.

"Thank you, Alli. Back at you."

"I'm all right Tim." She smiled a wide beautiful smile. Tim was floored with her beauty. Now she squeezed with both hands.

"This is unlike anything the surface world has ever known. We are feudal compared to the Granitarians and they know it. We were brought in because Cutter is one of ours. But for some reason when I don't hear from them, I feel like we're out of our league. This is too far above us."

Tim listened carefully. He understood what she was going through, because he had been feeling the same way. However, he had his own thoughts about motive. Granitarian motive.

Call it a cops intuition, but he noticed a certain mannerism. Sometimes a look from Allis' Granitarian guide when they were on the saucer. He wasn't concerned or going to mention it. But it was one of those things a good detective logs. Instead, he tried to ask her the right questions. "What I can't understand, is why the Granitarians need anything from us. Can't they track Cutters movements when he uses "The Phenomenon" device?"

"I don't think so. It's the high end of their technology, and my guide has been, shall we say, guarded in information release. They won't even tell us their names. They are scared of us. I'm sure of that. Remember, I was at one of their full meetings. Granitarians are frightened of being discovered by us. No matter what, they're still humans. With human frailties. They understand their own vulnerability."

Tim leaned back in the kitchen chair. For a moment he contemplated what she had just said. Then, leaned forward with a smile. "So they're frightened of us. I believe you. This highly advanced civilization that have flying saucers. If we saw one without knowing what you and I know, we might think they were aliens!"

Alli could see he was going somewhere. Tim had begun to rub his chin.

"They're aliens and we're just ants on the ant hill.....and yet, you are the one person out of everyone on Earth they invited to their cavern. Are you sure they're not secretly hoping to interact with the surface? If they don't need you, why did they choose you?"

Alli's smile disappeared. Tim's words hit like a freight train. Why did they choose her? It was a huge step for them to disregard their own laws and ask for help. She had always thought it was luck or what the Granitarian said. That she had a certain skill set. Could it be something else? Could there be a darker reason? Was she being used? Her gut told her no. That could not be. She shook her head. "What am I suppose to say to that, Tim. They know me, they know things about me? How could that be?"

Tim smiled and said, "I have some weird ideas, don't I."

"Don't mess with me Tim, this is too important."

"I'm not messing Alli. That comment was strickly professional. Like you said, this is extraordinary. Anything is possible! We must think outside the box."

Coffee turned into a walk around Allis' neighborhood. The conversation leaned toward small talk. The old Phoenix area was a favorite of Alli's, and Tim enjoyed seeing where she grew up. When they returned home, Alli kissed Tim on the cheek. He gave her a hug and returned to his truck. It had been a memorable evening for both, but tomorrow was a work day.

Chapter 22

After receiving more information concerning the father who allegedly murdered his wife and kids, Alli thought their conclusions were flawed. More importantly the Kingman police were looking for the wrong suspect. As she read through the report, certain witness statements caught her eye.

People in his neighborhood said he was a great dad. He worked as a big-rig mechanic for one of Kingman's many truck stops. Kingman, AZ. is just south of Las Vegas and a well known crossroads of interstate travel. Gas, food. Sometimes overpriced, but a wonderful town with lots of history. Though interstate highways carry a certain unwanted element, Kingman had a surprisingly low crime rate. There was nothing in the Kingman report that suggested foul play by the dad. However, he had disappeared. It made him an obvious suspect.

One aspect of the crime scene was that DNA from the father was all over the house, but of course that would be expected. He lived there. What they did not find, was strong amounts of his DNA on the victims. Minor traces, but his wife had defensive wounds on her arms and hands. In most cases she would have picked up DNA from the killer. There was none. So outside of the casual DNA from the father, the police could not use that science to convict. For Alli, that was an important detail.

The report did mention that none of the neighbors saw him come home after work. That was totally uncharacteristic of the man. He was a nine to fiver, and his 2005 F-150 was not in the driveway. The authorities found it parked at work. Subsequently the police figured he stole other transportation and murdered his family. Thus setting up an alibi. He was at work or went down the street for a drink. Anything that made it look like he never went home. The Kingman police were thorough. They checked the bars and talked to his co-workers. No one went out for drinks that night. This did look bad for the husband and father. Yet Alli was interested in other details.

One witness mention a blue van driving by the murdered families home. It was two or three days prior to the murders. No one got a look at the license plate number, but the driver had long hair. Probably a woman. She was driving alone. There was no one in the passenger seat. The witness was sure of that. But there could have been someone in back, out of sight. They saw the van twice in one day. It came up the street and slowed when it reached the mechanic's home. Though there was only one witness to the van, Alli believed this was the killer. A woman was stocking him!

Alli called the Kingman police and told them to look for old high school girlfriends that still lived in the area. The husbands age, from the same school and unmarried. Alli believed it was an ex-lover jealous of his life with his bride and children. He was probably kidnapped. Drugged, then thrown in her van and taken away. She may have had help. Someone sympathetic to her cause. Possibly another woman. She may have known him at work and had watched him for years. Alli also felt he was most likely still alive.

The Kingman, Arizona police were somewhat surprised with her profile, but took her advice and followed her line of thinking. The key would be the blue van. In Kingman it shouldn't be hard to find. Providing it had not left town. If they found it, they would let her know.

Allison "Alli" Chapman's skills of deduction were well known in the southwest. She just had a knack. A touch of genius method. Determining facts and result. Tim Renolds recognized that trait early on.

"Her, who done it? Was pretty skilled." He would say.

The Kingman Police obviously thought the father had gone insane. Killing his family and leaving town. But this man was a home town guy. Kingman has thousands of truckers and tourists coming through every day. This was personal. The long hair of the driver could have been a man, But in this case, it was a woman. Possibly two. Heavily armed. Premeditated. Very motivated. Alli was good at her trade. She believed she was correct. Now it was up to the Kingman Police.

Alli promised to help the Kingman authorities. It was an interesting case. She hoped the missing father could be found and exonerated.

She went about her day, doing paper work. Catching up on old cases and doing her normal. FBI work was not always glamorous. But it kept her busy while their plan for Cutter came to fruition.

Law enforcement agencies world wide, used the internet to coordinate their computers.. Linking all crimes to "The Phenomenon." Hoping to see a pattern in Cutter's M.O. (Method of operation.)

If there was a bank robbery, they looked into it. Any type of military crime, done by civilians. Double checked. Guns stolen from someone's home. Triple checked. Especially if the residents were still alive. Or even if they were dead, but not left in "The Phenomenon's" pose. It could be Cutter's doing.

Unfortunately, nothing came together. No connections. Suspects were either caught for their crimes. Processed and released. Or generally dismissed.

The murders were, of course, unusual in their nature. Law enforcement around the world was instructed to watch, and report, the unusual. This was not something authorities were unaccustomed to. The supernatural was part of their lives. Even if they just took reports. Tim Renolds thought there should be more instruction. It should be added in their morning orders. BOLO for everything weird. He knew the risk was an officer actually encountering something. Like a floating person. It could cost the officer his life.

Before Alli left for the day, Alli checked her computer for any word of the "Unusual." It had become a daily routine. There was the usual. - Might have seen someone fitting Cutter's description in Spain, or Belize. - They were interchangeable. Both came up all the time. Alli always searched under the heading "Unusual Occurrences." That was the world wide cop speak for "The Phenomenon." This was fresh protocol code name to help weed out the fanatics. The world still knew Martin Cutter as "The Phenomenon" killer.

She logged off and left the office at 4pm. The temperature was one-hundred degrees in Phoenix. Although it was hot, Alli pulled into a grocer and stepped out of her car. There standing in front of her was her pale friend.

Although surprised, Alli composed herself, quickly!

"Where have you been?" She asked softly.

"We are very proud of you Allison. How would you like to see more of the city tonight?"

"Would I!" They got back into Allis' car, waited for an elderly lady to walk by, then disappeared in a flash! Moments later, they stood in the center of Granitaria! It was called the "Old Section." There were smaller, older style apartment buildings. Separated by walking paths, like the rest of the city.

There were no vehicles. No other forms of transportation. Everyone walked.

Alli turned to take in the "Old Section." She breathed deeply and took in the slightly musty odor of the cave.

"I can't believe I'm here again! I've thought about Granitaria ever since I was here before."

"That is what happens. The allure of our home. What you are experiencing is not unlike what Cutter experienced. The difference is you are here by permission. We wish it. And, you're not insane!" Alli laughed at her companion and turned all around to see the city. It was beautiful! People in their multicolored jump suits exchanging greetings and going about their business. In the distance, modern, taller buildings. A lot of them. Bathed in incredible light. Some yellow and orange, others deep blues and reds. It was a wonder land. The taller buildings were like the one she stayed at on her first trip.

They walked to what seemed to be the center of Old Town. Toward what looked like a small lake. As they got closer, she could see all the way down. The water was crystal clear! Alli could see algae in all the colors of the rainbow running around the edge. It was one giant spring!

"We found this spring when we first came here. Our ancestors built their homes because it was here. It was much smaller then."

There were no words from Alli. Anything she could say would not be enough.

A man in overalls walked by singing lyrics that announced that the harvest was in, and to come to the market for the freshest of fruit. Lyrics that had been passed down for hundreds of generations. Father to son. Alli remained speechless.

There were stalagmites coming up from the floor of the cavern. Alli saw one patch that reminded her of the Painted Desert in Arizona. Ancient, layered in pastel colors like natural urban art. They made her feel comfortable. A moth flickered by and her guide reached out and grabbed it. He held it up for Alli to look at, then released it.

"That was quick!" Alli remarked. "On the surface, your people have a moth, called Granitaria!"

"Lets go on Allison., I have something to to show you."

The Granitarian and his guest walked to a new section of the city. He escorted her toward a square, one story structure. An it looked out of place, considering the tall sky scrapers around it! The doors opened automatically.

"This is one of our training facilities." Alli entered the building, and was amazed at what she saw. A large room completely open, filled with objects of different shapes and sizes.

There didn't seem to be any order to them. Like giant children's toys that needed to be picked up before Dad got home.

"We will play a game Alli! I want you to walk in that direction until you reach the middle of the room."

Alli began walking, stepping around different objects. Some round, some square, and some even sharp looking. Poles were sticking out of the walls, and there were small barriers in certain places.

When she reached the middle, she stopped.

"Is this OK?" Alli turned so she could face the Granitarian.

At that moment, the lights went out! It was pitch black! Alli was a bit frightened, but kept her cool.

"Are you all right Allison?"

She responded with, "How do I get out of here, without breaking my neck?"

"Listen to me carefully. Walk three paces forward, and turn to your right."

She repeated his instuctions.

"Walk three paces forward, and turn to the right? How far?"

"Just listen to me, and do what I say. You're fine. Now, walk forward eight paces and stop. Reach out with your hands. Can you feel it? Good. Step over the obstacle in front of you. Now walk three more steps and duck under a rail in front of you."

Alli Chapman was catching on to this game.

"Now walk straight ahead and stop. Turn to your left and feel for a large smooth object directly in front of you."

Alli felt a large smooth pillar.

"Now feel around it, following to the right. Keep going. That's it, Stop! Now turn around keep turning, stop. Now walk forward."

His voice increased in volume as she got closer.

The lights came on. She was right back where she started.

"How did you do that?"

"You call it sonar. WE learned it from the bats."

Alli was speechless.

"For several generations we have worked and lived in utter darkness. It was a natural sense to develop. It makes me happy to share with you. Share parts of our lives. I know you and your detective are frustrated by the enormity of what we ask of you. In our history, you will be legend."

Moments went by while two people from different words stared at one another. In those few seconds, Alli felt so proud. She was honored to be there. They had to succeed. The entire world depended on it. Two worlds.

Cutter was the weapon. He became that the moment he stole The Phenomenon device. He was a biological H-bomb. The resources of the world had to come together to destroy him.

Before they walked out of the training facility, Allis' guide made a gesture over an electric eye on the wall. All the pieces in the room randomly changed place for the next user.

As they walked back toward the spring, the guide took her hand. It was time for serious thoughts.

"The surface population can never know about us, Allison."

"My God, do you read minds, too?"

"No. But it would be natural for you to make comparisons to your world. For instance, What if we could exchange technology? The surface world could be helped by such advancements. Does this sound familiar?"

"Yes." She felt a little embarrassed. Her pale companion was very intuitive.

"I know that can't happen, but there's a lot of pain up there. I don't see it ending any time soon. Why can't surface humans see the warning signs and act on them? From what I've seen in my professional life, people would rather stick their heads in the sand and not respond to the evil around them. I wish I could go back up there and scream to the heavens. I'd tell them all about you. Granitaria could be the inspiration that jump-starts peace on the surface. But I know my place. As does Tim. Your secret will stay with us until the end of time."

"Your passion is wonderful. I wish you could scream to the heavens. But you'd have to be heard through several miles of rock."

"Alli let out a laugh. Her guide cracked a big smile. Moments later, her laughter came back, and repeated throughout the cavern. It lasted for almost a minuet. It repeated over, and over. It was a pivotal moment in their relationship.

When the laughter stopped, her smile faded.

"Don't make me go home. I love it here."

I know, Allison. You're envious of our way of life. You wish it for your people. That's what Granitaria does. It makes you wish."

"I know, I can't stay here. There's too much to do up there."

Her guide never told her his name. But she knew a lot about him. His instructions were always helpful. He never lied. Since that day on her driveway, he was her friend.

"A parting thought, Allison. The surface will some day be what you envision. But it will take many lifetimes and many lives. I'm sorry, but that is how it will unfold."

His words cut deep. Of course he was probably right. It occurred to Alli that her guide could actually see the future. But what he was saying, was just good old common sense. One thing was for sure. Earth's surface population was not ready for Granitarian technology. There would be governments everywhere trying to steal from Granitaria. It would lead to mass murder and war.

"Allison, it's time for you to return. Remember, Cutter is an egocentric maniac. He thinks he's invincible. He thinks he can't loose. Use it. Broadcast it. He has seen you. You have seen him. Your a liability. He will probably seek you out.

Find a place you can defend, and let him know where it is. You will succeed."

Alli soaked in every word. When she reached out to touch him, she was back in her car.

Chapter 23

Alli got a great education. Her father started saving for her when she was young. Not much. A little each month. Becoming an agent was her main focus after high school. She became a scientist and a marksman. A skill she was very proud of. Her sharp shooting coach at Quantico, rated her in the top one percent. She obtained degrees in Forensic Science, and Psychology. However, science, not to mention reality, had changed. Starting the moment a pale man appeared in her driveway.

Agent Chapman found she was bearing a heavy weight. Another dimension. A separate layer had been added to their lives. Beyond anyone else in the world, the two detectives kept a secret. A secret that changed Geology, Anthropology, History, and probably Math and General Science as well. The history of the Earth, was not what we thought. A secret? What a secret it was.

Of course Alli told Tim about her second trip to Granitaria. He was fascinated and jealous. But not surprised. If the Granitarians had wanted him there, they would have asked. No. The guide wanted to see Alli alone. Alli was the reason all of this was happening. If she had not been chosen, he would have never known about Granitaria. This reinforced his hypothesis. He felt he was absolutely correct. Something connected Alli to Granitaria. But for now, he would keep his thoughts to himself. It was not the right moment. Besides, he had planted the seeds of "Weird Ideas" in her head. Her reaction told him she, at least, partially believed him.

Allis' kitchen had become their confessional. They grew close there. But now it was time for war. They had to find a stronghold. The perfect location for the final battle. It was time for the second phase of their plan. The Granitarian guide laid it out for them. Bombard the airwaves with insults and kill Cutter when he showed his face. From now on, they had to make correct decisions. Every move they made, had to be the right one. Cutter was insane. That made him unpredictable. Whatever they came up with, had to be just as unpredictable. Location was key. There were a lot of variables. It was time to buckle down.

Chapter 24

A process began. Developing the battle plan to defeat Martin Cutter. The Phenomenon Killer.

The detectives could only suggest, not insist. He join them for the final battle. He had the advantage. So locating the perfect battle ground was essential. It could balance the scales. Put him off balance. Anything to stop him. Cutter had to believe the detectives were a real obstacle. He had to show up.

"Lure him in. Never let him out." Tim thought somewhere inside was best. An abandon building or warehouse. Cutter would be drawn in and that would be the end of it. That idea was kicked around until Alli pointed out the safety factor.

"We have to minimize collateral damage." She said. "Don't you want to use explosives?"

A remnant of Tim's military training. He was really good at making bombs. Small. Large. No matter. It was a gift.

It had to be a rural location. Then Tim could blow up everything. Without fear of injuring innocents.

Nothing was left out of the conversation. It had to be the right place. It had to be perfect.

The holy confessional of Allis' kitchen, had become their war room. US and state maps found their place on the floor. With a knock at the door, important materials were delivered. Beer and pizza. Mandatory for planning a war.

"All right, girl. Where are we going?"

Alli stood over the maps, pointing her finger from above. Removing her shoes, her toes became the pointer.

Texas was discussed. Oklahoma was looked at. Remote parts of Arizona were favored at first. But their home state was dismissed quickly. Arizona may have a lot of desert, but there are a lot of people in that desert.

No. It had to be somewhere people would not go, unless invited. Somewhere defensible. Somewhere they could build a story around. To lure their pray.

"Nevada!" Tim yelled so loud, Alli fell back in shock.

"Nevada. That's it. I've figured it out. Wow. I've got it. Area 51. It's perfect." Alli was not sure he was serious, but something told her it would be tough to get permission for that place.

"No, Tim. But maybe somewhere else in Nevada. It has plenty of remote spots." She retreated to her stove for a cup of coffee. All at once, Tim jumped to his feet. Grabbing his scalp with both hands.

"I feel like a rookie. I can't believe I didn't think of this earlier. Alli, there's an old Department of Agriculture sub-station out there in the middle of no where." Alli returned to the maps and found Tim tapping his foot on the Nevada map.

"Alli, this is it. My boss used to tell me about this weird place he guarded when he was young. The DOA was growing experimental vegetables and grains. In reality, it was probably a biological station making stuff for removing body parts." He paused in his story to see any reaction from his partner. There was none. Only her blank stare. He continued.

"It's a single story building with a chain link fence around it. It's got razor wire on top of the fence. They were growing corn where corn don't grow. My boss loved to talk about it. He'd always say,

"I'm not supposed to talk about that old place because it's classified. But I don't give a crap." Tim finished the story in a harsh, gruff, voice. Trying to imitate his superior.

"It's multilevel, with a laboratory, and maybe even a bathroom. As soon as you see this place, you want to know what goes on there. It's totally out of place."

Alli laughed at her partner. She thought he was full of it, but entertaining.

"I like your story, Tim. We need to move on something. The DOA site sounds like a strong possibility, But I want to see it for my self. By the way, man are you X-Files. You're killing me."

"Ya, I know. But it's worth talking to Captain Sweet. If not the interior of the building, the fields are fenced and remote."

"Can we control our position there? Can we see him coming?" She asked. Tim shook his head.

"I don't know, Alli. Let's talk to Sweet and see what he has to say. His description of the DOA site was so detailed. From what I remember, It's perfect for our needs."

The rest of the evening was spent planning and telling stories. Eventually, Alli offered up her couch. Tim accepted with little argument. They had put away a six-pack.

Whatever their feelings for one another, it was kept in check. They both knew it was love. Inescapable love. It was growing every minute. Every day. They were allowing to happen. Watching Alli laugh. Dancing with her. Holding her hand. Tim wished they could jump forward. Past their professionalism. Past what they were about to do. Alli was beautiful, smart, and carried a gun. He liked all three. He laid on her couch, wishing she would come out of her bedroom and make love. She did not. As he fell asleep, one question ran through his mind.

"What if one or both of us don't come home?"

Images of her lying on the ground made Tim angry. He was a little drunk. So he turned his thoughts to the DOA site.

Though he had never been there, he went through military planning as if he had. Planting mines. Positioning weapons. He wanted both of them to come out alive.

Chapter 25

The next morning, Alli fixed breakfast. Her partner woke to the smell of bacon mixed with coffee. Exotic coffee she received the previous Christmas. She called it her never sleep again potion. Tim followed his nose like a hound from the couch to the kitchen. The food was delicious.

"I think we should retire and open a diner. I haven't had a home cooked meal in a long time."

"I'm too young to retire." She boasted.

"I know you are. You're not done being a warrior." Tim answered.

It was the weekend. Tim believed his boss would be at home. He called, and Captain Sweet told him to come right over. When they arrived, Sweet did exactly what Tim said he would do. Talk up a storm. For years to come, the Captain would be a constant part of their adventures. Whether in person, or behind the scenes. They would rely on his wisdom and friendship.

"Ya, that old place was weird. It sits out there at the junction of E.T. Highway 375 and the Nevada 6. When I was in the military, I had guard duty out there. It was boring as hell. But they let us go to Vegas once in a while. I don't know what you guys want with it. It's long been abandon."

"Oh, not much boss. I'm just looking for an out of the way place to take my girl here." Alli's eyes could be seen from Mars. She stepped in front of him, going nose to nose. Then she spun around to face Captain Sweet.

"Sir! That piece of government real estate, may be of some use to the FBI. At a later date. I was just interested in your story."

"Well then FBI agent, I am happy to have talked to you."

The detectives stayed for ice tea and Alli thought the Captain was wonderful. She learned that his wife had passed years back. His obvious admiration for her partner was heart warming. He reminded her of her own father.

Following the meeting, the duo landed at a cafe. Alli began by launching into a reprimand for Tim's cheeky comment.

"I'll get you back for that one, brother. Just looking for a place to take me? You're done. You won't know when or see it coming." Tim began to laugh until he saw the look on her face. It basically said, she would remove body parts. With that out of the way, the conversation returned to planning their mission.

"We'll go to the DOA site. I can leave within 48 hours." Alli was anxious to explore Nevada. Captain Sweet had sold her on it. In any case, it could give them a place to fall back on. If things got rough.

Who knew where this was leading. This battle could end up state to state. Country to country. But that's not what they wanted.

Captain Sweet's testimonial proved it's remote location. Perfect strategic value.

"If it meets our approval, we stay and order our munitions. Like you said, Tim. Everything first class military."

"I'll rig it like you can't believe. Every high tech weapon and explosive we can dig up. We'll make it look like the freaking President is showing up to personally capture Martin Cutter."

"I want a way out for you and me. Also, contact your friends in South America. I want the guns from the cave. They might come in handy."

Alli was impressed. Obviously Tim knew how to start a war.

"We should increase the radio, and television pressure. Call him names. Really piss him off." She announced.

"Absolutely. It's time to get the military involved, as well. But just in the logistics. I don't want them around when things get rough. We'll need trucks and lots of guns. C-4 explosive. As many pounds as I can get my hands on. Oh, and one other item. I want a helicopter. It will have to be out of sight, but I want it close."

"You've covered a lot of ground. Haven't you Tim? I'm impressed. This sounds like you're constructing a mouse trap. Cutter goes in, but comes out in a body bag. Am I close?"

"That's exactly what we're trying to do. Burn him out. It may take a while. Ready to do some sitting around? Once the site is outfitted, it could be quite a wait."

The concern Tim had, was getting men with supplies in and out as fast as possible. His contact would send an escort with the trucks and weapons. But after delivery, the soldiers had to leave as soon as they could. More men could mean more deaths. Unacceptable. It had to be strictly a drop off. Help set up the place. Then bug out! Hopefully before Cutter showed up.

Chapter 26

Alli was ready to leave the next day. Not two. She made two phone calls. One to Tim. Telling him to get a car to the airport. The second to A.D. Phillips. Announcing that she had to leave town, unexpectedly. She was following a lead on The Phenomenon case. It could not be helped. Before he could ask any questions, she pulled the old,

"I'm late for the flight. Check in later. Thanks so much." Then hung up on him. Phillips understood drop-of-hat exercises from his agents. He just wish he knew what the hell was going on.

The detectives flew to Las Vegas. Rented a SUV, and drove northwest. The DOA site was a clear mark on the map. Thanks to Captain Sweet. Highway 375 and the Nevada 6. Just up the road, out west. When they arrived, they found the location perfect for their needs. It was remote and protected.

The link fence was locked with a chain. As was the steel door on the front of the building. They cut both. Inside they found a desk with a lamp, but no power. The dust said no one had entered for years. On a wall was a circuit box. Tim flipped the main circuit and the complex came to life. Lights came on. Inside and out. The elevator doors opened automatically. Inside, a single fluorescent bulb flickered. Sticking her head in the elevator, Alli took a quick look around. She caught a chill when it reminded her of a B horror movie. She pulled back quickly.

"There's a lot to explore." She said. Trying to diminish the goose bumps.

"The interior will have to wait." Tim agreed. They returned to the front gate. Tim retrieved two clip boards from their truck. One of the important chores was mapping the fields.

"Remember, Alli. Use the grid method. Make a mark where the soldiers should place the C-4. It will give them a guide. I know this method is old school, but those guys will understand it. It will save us a lot of time."

"Got it!" She responded.

Alli began walking the wheat field. Marking her grid paper. Tim moved through the corn field. Marking his pages as well. All in all, it took about an hour to complete their survey. This was their purpose for being there. Move quickly, so they could make a serious assessment of the site. Then act. Time was everything. Alli thought the fenced in fields were great. Knowing what they were up against, They were a natural barrier against floating human beings. She stopped for a moment.

"This is unbelievable. I don't know if I can do this."

The old wheat stood on about half an acre behind the building. The road ran in front. The corn was farther back. Several working oil rigs pumped away. Making their tell tale scraping noise. Off in the distance Tim could see huge windmills. Their blades slowly turning against the breeze. He took in the smell of the desert. Scents he never noticed in Phoenix due to the odor of car exhaust. It was quiet. He liked quiet. Another sensation he was unaccustomed to. As he walked back to the building, Alli was coming down the road. She had finished before him and decided to explore. Alli waved and they met in front of the building.

"I love it out here." She said. "But I can't stop thinking about what we may go through." Tim stared at the mountains. A large predatory bird soared some miles away. Too far to determine it's species.

"I know. It's truly beautiful with the mountains out there." For a few moments the pair had no words. It was hard to imagine this place - a killing field.

"Let's go, Alli." The duo made their way to the elevator and stepped inside.

"Shall we pull back the curtain and see what our tax dollars are buying?" Alli was itching to explore the lower levels. Inside the elevator they found buttons for three levels. Level one was ground floor. Then B1 and B2.

"Let's do these in order." And with that Alli pushed B1.

When the doors opened there was a brightly lit hallway with large windows looking into two rooms. They strolled over to the first window and peered inside. "Laboratories!" Tim was relieved they were empty and benign. Upon entering they found the usual glassware and scientific hardware associated with a working experimental station, but nothing that told them what went on there. Tim noticed a folder trapped under a bookcase on the floor. He bent down and retrieved it. The dusty folder was empty. But in small print on the front it read, Top Secret- White Candle Project.

"Wow!" Tim's reaction was a clear warning to Alli.

"I don't believe it." He said. He held the folder up for her to read. When she saw the title, she grabbed it out of his hand. At the same time she reached for her gun. Her instinct for fright and protection.

"What the hell is this? I don't believe in coincidence."

Alli studied the orange triangle with a burning candle in the center. The chosen color obviously designed to warn and intimidate.

"What the hell? The Granitarians had to know we would find this. It's evidence! It's us."

"What's going on here, Alli?" Tim reached for her shoulder. But she pulled away. Slamming the folder down on the lab bench. Knocking a glass beaker to the floor. She was angry. Embarrassed. Tim was there to witness her anger. Any perception of dishonesty connected to the Granitarians was unacceptable. Alli gave the folder a nudge and it floated to the floor.

"Damn, it. How could they have known?"

"It's all right, Alli. They've just tried to prepare us. It doesn't matter. They're more advanced than we are. We can't keep up. We're not supposed to. We'll never completely understand their motives."

"But we picked the DOA site." She said. "We never told them about it. We don't have to ask their permission.. They're not our freaking gods!" Alli's feelings were hurt. She trusted her friends. She trusted the Granitarians. She trusted her guide.

No doubt, White Candle was real. Probably a threat. Granitarians explained. As they said. Something to watch. Alli felt in her pocket for the protection device. Was it that simple? Were they led there? Could the Granitarians force a mental connection? For a moment she struggled with her commitment. Especially with her guide. She didn't even know his name. The charade of using a lawyer to deliver messages made her feel used. Like here's a clue children. Now go find the killer. They wouldn't do that, she thought. She took a few breaths. She knew damn well the Granitarians were frightened of being discovered. The majority wanted nothing to do with surface. In earlier discussions, non- answers were answers. Especially aboard their ship.

She had to remain loyal. They had to solve the case. These murders were horrible. Some might believe, biblical. As far as White Candle. It would all come out reveal. Secrets. Alli reached down and picked up the folder. It was evidence.

In the hallway of the laboratory level, the detectives contemplated how Cutter might come at them.

"What if he were to arrive down here?" Alli pointed down the hall, toward the labs. "If beamed directly from the surface, he could be floating in mid air. We have to be prepared for that." Tim placed his hand on the wall. "We could wire some C-4 on the walls and in the labs. Spider web trigger wire from floor to ceiling and dim the lights. He couldn't miss it!"

The duo returned to the elevator and proceeded to the remaining level. The doors opened and they stepped out. What they saw was surprising. A huge room with piles of corn and wheat. It was old. The grains had been there for some time. "I don't know what I expec- expected, but this wasn't it!" Alli was perplexed. "I don't get it. What's this place for? Were they planning on feeding the world?"

"It's super corn, Alli! Grows anywhere, feeds millions! I'm making this up as I go." Tim reached down and picked up a hand full of wheat. It had long ago lost it's golden color. He slowly poured it out of his palm, grumbling a few grains with the tips of his fingers. They walked around the piles for a few minutes, then when they turned to re-enter the elevator, Tim looked up to see the White Candle logo painted on the cement wall. "Oh, no." He said quietly.

Now Allison was very nervous about the warning from Granitaria. "How did they know, Tim? Are they preparing us for something terrible? I hate cryptic." They climbed aboard the elevator and returned to the surface. It was time to make a final decision before calling the military.

"We have to stay focused, Alli. I know we've seen a lot of weird stuff, but it's time to decide. Stick to the plan. Trust the Granitarians. I still believe you were singled out for this job. This is all about you." Although she felt a minor slice of betrayal, her gut had never lied. "My vote is yes. Let's go to work."

Tim grabbed his phone and hit speed dial. Moments later he was talking to his contact in the Army. "Ya, everything we discussed. The whole enchiladas. We'll be waiting." They walked out of the building and into the sunlight. It was warm.

"The sun feels good." She said. Alli looked east. Toward the road and distant mountains. She saw what was coming.

When the soldiers arrived, Tim put them to work wiring switches and placing explosives. Using the prepared maps, they moved through their jobs quickly. Tim and Alli began work on their camouflage blind. It would become their control central. A place of security. Somewhere to fall back to.

Tims' Army contact sent trucks and jeeps adorned with high ranking insignia, and lots of flashing lights. It helped create the atmosphere the detectives were looking for. In the middle of no where, something very important was going on. When it was time for the soldiers to depart, there was no argument. They had been briefed. They would leave on Tim's orders. After they were gone, Tim began placing his homemade explosives. Grenades taped to the top of poles. Four feet tall. It may have aroused suspicion from the experts. Why do it?

No reason for the explosive guys to see them. It may have aroused suspicion. Questions like, "Why are you doing that, Sir?" Or, "Sir, that's not the best use of a grenade."

The idea was simple. Anyone floating would be taken down. Hopefully, Cutter. Detective Tim put a lot of thought into this action. He felt sure it would be affective. Defend Alli. Protect them from attack.

When he was done, he found Alli putting the finishing touches on their camo blind.

"That looks great, Alli. From out here you can't see it." She looked up at him.

"This is hard work. Even with all the help. I hope it pays of. I want that bastard."

"It will." He said. "And I think it's time for phase three. It's time to call my boss."

Captain Sweet had no idea that he was to become an integral part of an FBI operation. Considering he was the Phoenix Chief of Detectives, this would be a neat trick.

"Hello, Boss. Greetings from Central Nevada. I've got an update for ya."

"So you decided to go check that place out?"

"We did. And we took it." Tim sounded like he was purchasing real estate.

Captain Sweet, on the other hand, was feeling pride he hadn't felt since he was in the service. With his favorite detective standing on ground he protected so many years before. Whatever they were up to, he was a part of it.

"What's the old place looking like these days?"

"Unused. Until now. We're ready for the next phase. I've got some instructions for a press release. If your ready? Boss?"

"It's your dime, son."

"Tell our contacts there's a task force being set up in Nevada. Specifically to capture Martin Cutter. It's in west central Nevada, and has the latest in surveillance and tracking technology. High ranking military are in command. Along with two Arizona detectives. Fill in our names. We've seen the SOB. We're betting on the fact he doesn't like loose ends. He'll track us, and walk into our trap."

Captain Sweet finished taking notes. He considered pressing Tim on their encounter in Peru. But instead he asked,

"I take it, these messages need to be run 24/7?"

"Absolutely. This is a one time deal, boss. We have to push him hard enough to kill us. When he's had enough, he'll come calling."

"Is this all you think I'm good for? Playing press secretary? I want in on the fight!"

"Mmmm, not this time, boss." Tim would love to have his Captain along, but not for this one. This was different.

"I'm just kidding. I know what you need, kid. I'm taking notes while we've been talking. Anything else?"

"Just hit the airwaves. Broadcast world wide. Don't let up. Alert the media. Military. Hell, tell the weather channel. It's time to tell everyone. Cutter has to find us on his own. The media is already calling him a coward. Step up that angle. Alli and I left prepared statements in my desk drawer. If anything happens to us. There's a lot we can't tell you. But our profile says he's got an ego the size of Texas. In Peru, we got his weapons stash. It ruined his plans. Or at least slowed him down a bit. He doesn't like that. That's our angle."

"Ok, kid. I'll get right on this and get back to you when I've lined some things out."

"Thanks, Boss. You're the best." Tim hung up the phone, looked at Alli and raised one eyebrow.

"Here we go." He said. It reminded her of someone. But she couldn't remember who.

"Who raises one eyebrow? Who does that, Tim?"

He just smiled, and said.

"Think about it. I'll give you a hint. He's not from around here," and he just wants to "Live long and prosper."

Chapter 27

"Hurry! Come. There is someone here."

"What? What do you mean?"

"There is someone here. Maybe from above."

"That's impossible."

"I think he's injured."

Making a sharp turn in the cave, four cave dwellers catch up to their friend. They are explorers. The caves in this area had not been previously mapped. Finding anyone there was quite unexpected. On the floor of the cave was a strange man. He was bleeding and unconscious His unusual clothing told them he was not one of their people. Above him was a large whole in the Earth. Fresh dirt and rock surrounding him proved he had fallen through.

"Is he alive?"

"Yes. Barely. What are we going to do?"

"Leave him." One of the cave dwellers proposed.

"Let him die. It's not our place to make this type of decision. We must go back and tell the others."

For a moment there was silence while the five connected their thoughts. A capability they had developed over thousands of years. In the end, compassion won the moment.

"It's settled then. Bind his wounds. We'll pick him up. Carry him as far as we can." The man had wounds to his leg and chest. Possibly a broken rib or two. Breaking into their supplies, they patched him up. Then two aside, one holding his head, they began the long track home.

Several days later a man and woman sat next to a bed. The man they found in the cave was showing signs of regaining consciousness. He would not be able to move for some time. But his eyes began to open.

"Hello." The woman said softly. "Can you hear my words?"

The injured man had a sharp gruff voice.

"Where the hell am I? What happened?" This time, the woman's partner responded.

"We found you in one of our caves. You were badly hurt. You've been asleep for some time." The man twisted on his bed, Trying to get up.

"No! You mustn't. You're in no condition. You must stop!" The cave dwellers, held him down. Then with the swipe from an instrument just above his forehead, he fell unconscious.

"He's very strong. We should bind him." They did.

"We should alert the others that he is awake. Some will be very angry."

In the weeks and months that followed, Martin Cutter would heal. The first time he got out of bed and realized where he was, he fell to his knees. He sobbed like a child. His first reaction was of horror. His ignorance wouldn't allow him to be amazed.

After a few days, Cutter lost some of his fear.

"They were so nice." They treated him well.

But he still saw them as foreigners. Like in a foreign country. Where his prejudice could kick in. In time, though, the great cavern's intoxicating effect, took over. He had found his city of gold. It was all his.

"They're simple. Easily manipulated. But I need help."

"I can rule this place."

However, there was a slight problem. Whenever he brought up returning to the surface, no one would tell him how. Many times he located caves leading away from the city. But always he would return. Getting lost or turned around. Again and again he confronted different Granitarians. He was always met with silence. Then one day he was walking near a training facility. One of the crystal walls was clear enough to see in. A woman holding a small device was turning knobs and pushing buttons. A man facing her began to rise. Soon, he was floating around the room. Dodging obstacles as he went. Sometimes floating over. Sometimes under. Cutter was amazed. Suddenly, she began to float with him. It was at that point she saw

Cutter watching them. In a flash, the wall went dark and Cutter could no longer see them.

At this point, the Granitarians made two mistakes. One was underestimating Cutter's obsessive-compulsive need to obtain anything that could make him rich. The other was made by the woman. As if she flew through the wall, in an instant she stood next to him. Her next statement told Cutter everything he needed to know.

"What are you doing here? This place is off limits to you."

"Is it now?" Cutter replied. "I didn't see any signs." The woman's misunderstanding of surface slang just made things worse. The Granitarian was angry. This was something he was not suppose to see.

After that it was all he could think about. Whatever it was, he had to have it. In time, he would find maps showing the way up. That's when his plan came together. The original suggestion of leaving him in the cave to die was the correct one. When he reached the surface, he tried out his new toy. He had no instructions, so he just turned a knob. A woman near by immediately contorted and died. That was how Martin Cutter found he had the ultimate killing device.

The Granitarians greatest fears were realized. They had been too trusting. They let compassion out way their laws. They gave chase, but too late. The Granitarians treated him too good. Even advanced technology was second to being isolationists. It made them naive. By not letting him come and go as he pleased he stayed too long. Saw too much.

Now, months later he's had time to learn and perfect his craft. Cutter is only interested in revenge. A plan, based on emotion. Devised the moment he saw the Granitarian weapon.

The device was a terrible instrument. It provided stealth, multiple deaths, and instantaneous travel. All in one hand held machine. The Granitarians were correct to compare it to an atomic weapon. Imagine a war where a hand full of soldiers carried the device, and thousands of the opposition did not. There are no words in any language to describe the result. Cutter was an insane child wielding technology thousands of years ahead of anything on the surface.

The larger issue was he knew of their existence. By the time they realized what he had done, it was too late. He took the device and the maps and left their realm. In fact, at that very moment he was emerging from a small cave opening by clearing the debris himself. Against their better judgment, and in defiance of their laws, the Granitarians sent out a search party. It was quickly called off. They had no idea where to start.

Soon afterwards, the man that would become Alli's guide called his fellow Granitarians to the great meeting place. There he laid out a plan to have a surface dweller help with this matter. Naturally there was much opposition. But, what else could they do?

"The weapon must be returned. And immediately. Cutter will use it. Of that I have no doubt. Left on the surface it would become a scourge. Eventually, Cutter may loose it to someone else. Or have it stolen. As he did to us. It is too big a risk. Also, I know of someone who I believe is the right choice to assist us."

"How could you know of anyone on the surface?" A man asked.

Alli's guide took a long moment before he answered. Granitarians never lied. They were one clan. One family. Truth was what bound their laws together.

"She may be related to me."

Chapter 28

On the surface, Cutter had several hiding places. They were scattered around the globe. One of his favorites was Miami. He liked the sun and knew the city. His mother moved them there when he was seven. She was a prostitute. When paying customers came around, she locked him in the closet. Or sent him outside to fend for himself. His outlook on life was developed in those early years. Along with a lack of education, his path was set. All that was left was to fall through the social cracks and discover a race of advanced humans in a cavern. Not the story of the average serial killer, but like Jeffery Dolmer there had to be some motivator. Even he had parents. And an animal or two. Of all the surface humans that could have discovered Granitaria, it had to be someone like Martin Cutter. The snake in the Garden of Eden.

Loosing the cave in Peru infuriated Cutter. He returned after the FBI left. He found his weapons were gone. Though he had the ultimate weapon, he had plans for those..Shortly there after hundreds of locals descended on the cave claiming it's riches for their own. All via a phone call from an unknown person at the FBI. She felt she should give back. It was the twenty-first century thing to do. This just added to his insanity. At the time, Alli was just thinking of the Moche Indians. After all, it was their cave. She would never want to piss Cutter off. Heaven forbid. Besides, Tim's plan to make a stand at the DOA site came long after her phone call to tribal leaders of the Moche. In this matter she felt vetted. Now it turned out to be the perfect thing to do. Keep rubbing stuff in his face.

That was exactly what was needed. Constant bombardment of insults and innuendo. But much like elections, there were consequences. Like elections, the new guy brings in his people. Out with the old, in with the new. The rules change. Gloves come off. Wars get started. It can be argued that sanity and the ability to relate are the true cause of war. The side that is attacked finally says that's enough. Action - Reaction.

Chapter 29

Captain P.J. Sweet compared Tim to the great cops he knew when he was young. Men and women he worked with in the 1980's, when he was a street cop. If the higher ups at the FBI and the Phoenix Police Department wanted their people to work together, he would do whatever was needed to aid in the hunt. He was the right choice to get the message out to the media. First off, he hated them. Secondly, he knew how to pull their chains. Like politicians, making promises they would never keep. The press seems to like that. It doesn't remember when the promises are not kept. Captain Sweet listed that as one of his rules to live by. Cable news, the AP. The Times, and papers all over the world repeated the detectives narrative. That the authorities were hot on the trail of the coward serial killer Martin Cutter. He was "The Phenomenon" killer. A joint task force was being set up at a remote location in west central Nevada. Unlimited resources were being applied for his capture. Smiling photos of Alli and Tim, along side their sketch of Cutter, were insult enough. Add fuzzy tape of the trucks and personal at the DoA site, and it made for attractive bait! The sketch was a close likeness. When Cutter saw himself on television, he started breaking things in his apartment. He would not be able to stay in one place very long. Someone might recognize him.

In the high rise in Miami, Cutter tossed back beers and threw the empties at the fifty inch T.V. Anger was turning to obsession. Precisely what the detectives hoped for.

Chapter 30

Drinking until he passed out. Cutter's daily routine. All the power he possessed. Still he reverted to old habits. Visions of his law enforcement tormentors giving chase in the cave. His face on television. His own grizzly death. These nightmares began to take hold. Drunk and angry was the mixture, and hatred makes poison. Cutter was consumed. The detectives had to die. They cramped his style. He felt cornered. They had changed the conditions of the game. So be it.

His answer was to step up the carnage. Become more cruel. Use the stolen technology to kill the killers. Affect the DNA of one, have them kill three. Then fall off a building. Or be slammed into a wall. He became very handy with the Granitarian technology. His pawns were his puppets. Like killers before him, people were mere targets to practice on. Honing his skills for war. He wanted the world to burn. He wanted to punish families.

Cutter stepped out on his balcony. He began adjusting the device. He wanted to widen the field so it covered the entire high rise. Then pushed the master button. He had never tried this before. He wanted to see what would happen.

The terror of this weapon was it's silence. It selectively identified the correct DNA, then switched that individual on as the killer. With that they could float, touch, and kill. No one could hear them coming. That was it's special gift. Stealth.

Men, women and children began floating through the apartment building! At first, just within their own apartments. One family member killing the rest. Soon they were everywhere. With a touch, their victims went down into the posture of death associated with "The Phenomenon." Fifteen stories of building were effected. The pawns were everywhere. Floating outside windows, then crashing through! Cutting themselves on glass to reach their victims. There were so many they ran into one another. Down hallways, banging at doors, kicking at walls. When anyone opened to object, they were touched. Death was instantaneous.

Tenents owning fire arms, opened fire on their neighbors when they floated into their homes. Those that did not own a gun tried to shield family members with their own bodies. It did not work. Children screamed. Mothers screamed. It was terrible carnage. Just senseless tragedy. One of Cutter's pawns floated outside a window ten stories up. The owner shot through the window and hit his target. The man woke as he fell to his death. He did not understand. He did not know what he was doing there. By the time his mind comprehended that he was falling, it was too late. When it was over, the murderer was long gone. He had two cops to kill. He had left his mark. One hundred plus dead. Many others wounded or wandering the complex not knowing what happened or if their friends and relatives were alive. The real horror was reserved for the survivors. They had to clean up Cutters' mess. Their lives were over as well. None of them would ever be the same.

Now "The Phenomenon" was out of the bag! Anyone that survived the apartment attack, saw how it worked. People floated, then touched others and they died. It was horrible! The world was immediately alerted to the facts. "The Phenomenon" was the ability to kill. It could be anyone. Was it some new technology? Was the government behind it? What could possibly give someone the ability to do this? Aliens? The rumors never stopped.

By the time the news of the Miami tragedy reached Alli Chapman, the detectives were making a final trip back to Phoenix for supplies. When they saw photos of what really happened. Photos too graphic for the public. Alli made an executive decision to pack up Tim and find an out of the way place to get drunk. Tim suggested a biker bar out on route 60. It turned out to be perfect for their needs until they found themselves back at her house the next morning. Unable to explain how they got there. Both had a few cuts and bruises, again unexplainable. When Alli sobered up and climbed into a hot shower, she began crying uncontrollably. The photos of Miami ran through her head. They made her sick. Sadness turned to anger and determination. They would not fail.

Chapter 31

News of the apartment murders went viral. It was like the second coming. The most important news ever reported. Washington bureaucrats immediately weighed in, claiming the technology must be from a foreign government. Not from the United States! There was even some theater when an aid to a Senator approached the podium during a press conference. He passed the Senator a note to help him explain away any U.S. involvement.

"Oh, yes, here we are. It's been confirmed. This isn't United States technology. No, we wouldn't have anything like this." Of course it was all lies. No one outside Alli and Tim had any idea what was happening. Following the Senator, the director of the FBI went to the podium. His words proved his ignorance.

"We are taking the appropriate steps to find and subdue Martin Cutter. A person of interest."

"Bull!" Tim flipped off the television. "Alli, they don't have a clue. Cutter killed those folks in the building to get back at us." Alli leaned out of the kitchen.

"I know. We made him react. But his reaction was so damn harsh." Wiping her hands, she joined Tim on the couch.

"The politicians want in on the latest game of the century. It's our game, but they want the cameras turned on them. Like the cartoon said, "How do we keep them looking at us now?" Tim smiled and shook his head.

"Freaking liars!"

Alli was concerned there'd be pressure from Washington.

"This could get sticky, Tim. I can't wait till my boss starts in on me for up dates. Your boss is cool and he's been partially read in on this. But my boss is probably getting heat from the White House. I don't need him asking questions."

Another concern was the Granitarians. Would they become more active now that Cutter was moving to genocide?

"From our perspective, Miami was the worst thing he could have done. It was an escalation that we didn't need." As the detectives sat on the couch, both had symptoms of remorse. Part of their plan had been accomplished. But Cutter killed so many all at once. What would he do next? What would be the Granitarian response? Their secret was in jeopardy.

Cutter was on the move. Using the Particle Highway system to many cities around the world. He killed only once. In Venice, Italy he thought two people had recognized him. Whether they had or not, he killed three to eliminate two. Days later he arrived back in the states, finding a hiding place in Dallas. A small vacant ranch on the outskirts of the city. The owners on vacation. Lucky for them. It had a long driveway that curved back to the main house. From there he could watch for anyone coming.

With the experiment in Miami, Cutter had proven the power of the device. He was achieving larger, more dramatic events. Now he really knew his technology. Until now it had not been explored. He would not need to continue the small stuff. It was the large scale terror attacks that got the worlds' attention. But the media was still touting the authorities. His tormentors got all the positive press. With head shots of Alli and Tim on billboards and news programs reading statements claiming to find, and destroy Martin Cutter. Something had to be done. He would never achieve his goals while they were alive.

After two days in Dallas, Cutter heard a prepared statement from FBI agent Allison Chapman. It read,

"Detective Tim Renolds and I are part of a multi-agency task force being housed in west central Nevada. It's sole purpose is to bring to justice the coward serial killer, Martin Cutter!" That was it! That is what Cutter was waiting for. They showed their hand. He was going to Las Vegas! But he had one more task to perform.

Chapter 32

At eight o'clock Zurich time, the bank manager of the Zurich National Bank unlocked a side door to allow employees to enter. He was very patient, unlocking the door for each. Then re-locking it for security. This was done on time every day. He was never late.

The vault was on a timer. It required two keys to be inserted at exactly eight-ten am. The locks were on either side of the great door. It took a second employee to turn the keys at the appropriate moment. She would arrive exactly five minutes prior, to prepare. Certain schedules had changed through the years, but not this one. This was an old bank steeped in tradition.

At eight-ten am, the keys were inserted and turned. The vault door swung open. The large amount of cash that usually sat in the middle of the floor was gone! Two million American dollars. The manager uttered vulgarities and ran from the vault. They had been robbed.

Cutter had been there. He came and went several times during the night. Each time filling duffel bags full of cash. It felt safer to rob northern Europe than the U.S. He traveled to four different banks in search of U.S. currency. Zurich National was very accommodating. He needed play money for Las Vegas. He planned on having a couple swinging nights before he had to go to work. In addition, large sums of money to throw around for business. Maybe some large purchases. He had big plans for his future.

The authorities lacked evidence to explain the crime. The door of the vault was never opened. Never the less the money was gone. Embarrassed, they blamed the "Phenomenon Killer" They were right of course. Cutter would later brag to some Las Vegas showgirls that this was his "Nobel Prize." Given to him for his humanitarian work.

He had a plan. A plan to kill two cops.

Chapter 33

Tim made a final walk around. With the last bit of sunlight he checked his explosives. Just inside the main gate and along the fence, he left a pathway. Clear of explosive traps. It gave them an escape. If for any reason they needed to flank the road, there was an unencumbered exit.

Under the corn and against the fence he placed a handgun and extra shotgun. The shotgun at Alli's request. If they were compromised, they had a retreat. For a moment Tim thought about the Space Station. Under his breath he said,

"That freakin guy. Just come and find us. Will be here."

Alli sat in the camouflage blind, feet propped up, cleaning her automatic weapon. She made sure to hit the firing range before they left Phoenix. She wanted to be sharp. The detectives did a good job on the camo-blind. It was reinforced with brick on all sides. The interior was lined with flack vests. Innocuous looking bushes and sage surrounded the exterior. Even from the road you would not notice the blind. The vehicles were parked all around. It blended right in. It was command central and housed the night vision monitors, flood light switches, and digital triggers for the explosives. Most of all, it was a safe haven for the two people trying to save their nation. They had been given a gift of knowledge. No matter what, it spurred them on. In her heart and soul, Alli prepared for what would come after. An epic battle. With a great awakening at the end. Both she and Tim secured a great secret. But in the future could the Grantarians keep their secret? Or would it be forced to the surface by human curiosity? Alli was afraid of questions that might arise to explain details. The technology was certainly other worldly. What did they know about it?

Then there was this vague mention of something called White Candle. Like her guide said, "The candle in the triangle is an action started by humans on the surface." He called it by name. How could he know? Granitarian knowledge was vast. But where White Candle was concerned, she longed to learn more. Was it a threat to national security? Was it our own government? The answers would have to wait. There was a job to do.

The detectives focused on assorted radio frequencies and night vision monitors. Monitoring Captain Sweet's radio blurbs was a blast. He was very creative.

"When law enforcement confronted Martin Cutter down in Peru, he ran away. Just two detectives chased him out of a cave he was hiding in. He ran away. He's a coward!"

It was also time to perform the age old police task of sitting around. Waiting for something to happen. It was a hard sell, too. With the nightly party in Vegas just down the road. Tim thought about packing Alli up and hauling her off to the strip. Cutter be damned. It was a nice thought, but a scenario not likely to take place. His fantasy of making love to Alli in a Mandaley Bay bed would have to keep.

He had been asked to work security at a Las Vegas hot spot one summer. It was life changing. It was after that he went back to Phoenix and became a cop. Tim thought about that for a moment. He realized it was that time in Vegas that brought him to all of this. He was fresh out of the Army when he went to Nevada. Now he is involved in the most important investigation in the history of man. Funny how things turn out. Then he laughed.

"Wow! Aliens are real!"

Around ten-thirty pm, some kids to young for the casinos cruised Flamingo Boulevard. One of them looked up and saw a bright, triangular light some distance away. The lights of Vegas are so bright it was hard to focus on, but it was something. Then in the blink of an eye, it was gone. The teen was so surprised, he yelled out.

"Hey! Did you guys see that? It was a plane or something. Then it just disappeared!" His friends were like, "Whatever dude. Probably just some jet out of McCarran!"

"Ya, well I think it was something else." He was right. His friends would soon change their tune.

Chapter 34

"What the hell is that?" A couple from Wyoming were shocked at what they saw. "It's coming our way. Get your cell phone, honey. Get some shots!" All over Las Vegas people turned their eyes to the sky. From the south came a large saucer shaped craft. It lazily tracked up Las Vegas Boulevard, causing great concern with the tower at McCarran Airport. They could clearly see it. Whatever it was could interfere with local air traffic. It moved so slow, some thought it might land. Then with a burst of speed, it parked right over the Horseshoe Casino. An old woman was knocked down when people scrambled to get outside for a look. She was immediately picked up. All the while screaming at her good samaritans to let her see the flying saucer! It looked real. Then in another burst of speed it left Fremont Street heading northwest. It gained altitude as it left Las Vegas airspace. They had just had their own "Phoenix Lights Case!"

Minutes later four FA35 fighter jets were scrambled from Nellis A.F.B. They passed over Las Vegas in the same general direction. The ship was long gone, but the jets made a go of it anyway. The news media and every cop in Nevada were on high alert. The craft was not threatening the population. At least not yet. It looked real and it scared some folks. Phones rang off the hook at police stations all over the county. Of course several calls were made to Washington, D.C. Too many had seen the "Ship." It would cause a stir, but these things tend to work themselves out.

Not long after the FA-35's gave chase, they were told to stand down. The military was aware of the menace. They also knew they would never catch one. It would have to crash. Then maybe. Or maybe not. More than one old UFO file stated that a wounded UFO was helped by another. Both disappearing in the night. Besides. What would the government do if they shot this one down? So many people had seen it.

Allis' Granitarian friends were as they say in Vegas, hedging their bets. Lighting the way to the party. They had been watching.

Monitoring every move the detectives made. The Granitarians believed Alli was right. Setting a trap for Cutter in Nevada was the right approach. The fact they'd found supporting evidence of something called White Candle, was pure coincidence. The Granitarians were sure Cutter was near by.

"Go to stealth. We will stay and watch." Using technology one-third as old as the Woolly Mammoth, their saucer literally disappeared in the night.

Logic dictated that after the apartment attack in Miami, Cutter would have been out of control. Crazy with power. But he stopped. Very few "Phenomenon" related deaths were reported. His obsession with the detectives neutered his instincts. It was strange. An unexpected reversal of his M.O (Method of Operation.) Historically, when serial killers are not captured right away, they escalate. They only slow down or stop when the heat is on. Cutter stopped for a reason. He was stocking the detectives.

The Granitarians guessed correctly. Surface humans are very predictable. By showing the space craft, making their presents known, they were asking Cutter very simple questions.

"Do you want to be a ruler? Then it's time to act like one. Do you want war? Then let us have war."

In the days that followed, the civilians that witnessed the UFO became instant experts in all things paranormal. One man swore it stopped over his car and abducted his wife. That was just Las Vegas. Divorce courts are as busy as wedding chapels. Others would say it was a hoax. Some new "Come to Vegas!" promotion. That is just how these things worked. They always have. People will dismiss. Rather than believe. Even when it is right in front of their eyes.

Chapter 35

Silence. The DOA site was silent. So quiet. Like soldiers stories. No sound of insects. No sound at all. The wildlife had long since abandoned the area. Tim did not notice. But Alli did. She didn't like it. She didn't like being patient. It was gut wrenching. Like waiting for someone you don't like to come to your house. But that was the curse. Waiting for your enemy. It lends time to dark thoughts. Alli didn't do well with it.

The camouflage blind was complete. The DOA site was as protected as they could make it. It was wired to repel and destroy the enemy. Tim's design was defensive and offensive. He could run it with a click from a mouse.

Alli cleaned her weapons twice. Any more and Tim would have taken them away from her. Though the site had digital cameras everywhere, she kept staring out a hole in the canvas. Just in case.

Tim saw what was happening. He'd seen it before. Soldiers twitching in their seats. Rubbing their hands together. Eyes wide open. He reached for Alli's knee.

"What are you thinking about?" He asked.

"Nothing." She replied. "Nothing at all." There was a pause. Long enough for her to think of what else to say. Then she turned to him with a look of desperation.

"I don't like stake outs. Ok?" Tim smiled. He knew she was all right.

"Damn it, Renolds. I believe in a strong offense. But this case. We could chase this bastard all over the world and never catch him. I prefer chasing the bad guys. Not waiting for them to come to me. It lessons my sense of superiority."

Tim laughed. He couldn't help it. She did have an ego. She wasn't all sugar.

"I know." He said. "Sitting around sucks. You're a warrior. A great warrior." He turned back to the monitors. Picking up a cloth, he wiped off the screens. Again there was a pause in the conversation.

What he said to her, was the best he could have done. It made her feel warm, and needed.

"Tim, I'm thinking about Granitaria. How it's changed me. How it's changed us. I love it's beauty and sophistication. I feel like an addict. Somewhere in there is my hope of a peaceful life."

"Ya, I know. But this morning, stay sharp. I promise you. Someday. We'll have that."

What mattered was trust. It had always been hard for her. This was all so complicated. The Granitarians obviously controlled their population growth. For millenia, living in limited space. With limited resources. They developed a collective consciousness. It advanced their culture in ways the surface never could. When they chose not to leave the caves, thousands of years of peace followed. Now, interrupted by a megalomaniac.

Alli contemplated her world. The surface world. He home. So beautiful. So many possibilities. Yet, unbelievable ignorance. Her time in Washington, D.C. taught her to be wary. The lies. The imperfections. The untruths.

We are the freest land on Earth.

We truly lead our selves. But there's that pesky status quo. Politicians are only elected to be an extension of our true believes. But it doesn't last long.

She stood up. Behind Tim. She reached around him to give him a hug. In his ear, she whispered.

"Surface humans, Tim. We're part of them. What are we going to do with them?"

"My religion is the true religion. Kill you and your god."

"You have land I want. I'll take it from you."

"Countries on the surface, don't see eye to eye. They're all too weak. Our living area is so much greater than Granitaria. We can see the stars. We can see them and dream about them. Granitarians can visit them. How much time have we waisted?"

She was restless in the blind.

"Should I try and sleep?" She asked under her breath.

"Miami. Oh, God. Did we push him to that?"

Her father installed values in her that were suppose to be helpful. As much as she tried, only one stuck out. She could still hear his voice, as if he were there.

Accomplishments only matter when they were completed. The higher number of accomplishments, the less they mattered. It's back bone and bravery that matter most."

What was important now, was her home. The FBI. The nation, and in this case, the world. Obviously the Granitarians were the direct motivation. This case changed her life. Forever. But most of all it was Tim. Yes. Tim Renolds had to be included now. He mattered to her. His words. His touch. Making her realize things are not always what they seem. For instance. There was a strange familiarity with her guide. Ever since the second trip to Granitarian.

Alli sensed something about him. It was fleeting, but it was there. Standing by that beautiful, deep, spring. Tim noticed it first. That was disturbing enough. On the space craft. Something the guide did. Or something we did together. Tim stands back and sees things for what they are. These new people and new situations are my future. Especially my two new men. My guide because he molded me. Tim because I know he loves me."

She'd been falling in love since the day they met. It was all about truth. Truth about the "Phenomenon" case and truth between two people.

Granitaria changed her life. Everything started over when she was approached by the guide. Her life before stopped. A new one began.

"My own personal version of string theory." She thought. Something she would truly understand in the future. This was just the beginning.

She turned her attention back to the security monitors. Tim had walked outside. Something about a sagging canvas.

It was coming. Like the aches and pains you get when a storm is brewing. He was coming.

Chapter 36

Alli was a sharp shooter. Considered to be the best in her class. She had that extra sense. Her class mates called her "Third Eye." But that was lost along the way. During her time in the academy, there were boys. They lined the halls just like high school. Only these halls lead to gun ranges and forensic science classes. Serious people study. There's no time for B.S. Labels. Imposed by idiots, were never accurate. Especially were Alli was concerned. Her skills were about to be tested. Her love of life as well. She'd need all her strength to defeat this man. All her strength to protect Tim.

It was time for war. Time to battle advanced technology. It would be a defensive war. To win, they would have to turn the tables on Cutter. React quickly and shoot to kill.

Tim Renolds saw the whole business in black and white. His military training poured out of him. He repeated strategy over and over. Driving his points home to Alli. He was annoying. But she allowed him to have his say.

"He could come at us from the desert, Alli. Or as we discussed, Particle Bore directly into the building. Or behind it. He might come through the corn, but my toys might give him a hard time. He may try to flank us and come straight down the road from the north."

Alli made mental notes. Tim was very thorough. It was like he saw the battle before it began. They were prepared. Ready for war. It would be unpredictable and tragic, but they were prepared.

"Do you want to sleep? It's been twenty-four hours." Tim pointed to a cot in the corner of the blind. Alli looked up and shook her head. She sipped coffee from a thermos.

"Do you feel that?" She asked.

"You mean my gut talking to me? Like it's far off but coming just the same?"

As if the camouflage blind was suddenly filled with static electricity, waves of Adrenaline guaranteed there would be no sleep. This was it....They were proud to fight Cutter. For the Granitarians and their society. Like it should be. Brought together with purpose. For the world. People would never know what they did. The detectives were honored.

Tim glanced at his watch. It was six-thirty am. The glow of what would be a magnificent sunrise had just begun behind the mountains to the east. For a few moments he stared at his partner. If she had noticed the look on his face, she may have questioned what he was thinking. He thought she looked great in the morning. The most beautiful woman he had ever seen. Her brown hair pulled back. Wearing a dark sweater that zipped up the front. Over that she wore a black flak jacket. As did he. It masked her figure a bit, but damn she looked good!

Right then a sensor went off! On the back side of the building. Way out past the corn. Could it be an animal? They had not seen to many. A few birds. A couple deer. Maybe it was their pray. Had he taken the bate?

"Should I go?" Alli was ready. It was decided that she would play the part of rover and remain mobile. It was her style to act as a gorilla fighter, but Tim wanted her to hang on a little longer.

"No." He said. "Stay a while. Let the sensors track. We'll know if the alert is human. The longer you stay in the blind, the less likely you'll be caught out in the open."

There were no sounds. No distant rustling of corn or breaking of stocks. However, the sensors would hear everything. Even footsteps. Area 51 used the same sound sensing technology. Highly sensitive, and a must have for security.

Alli quietly loaded another shell into her pump shotgun. She brought her 308 as well. Her favorite for rapid fire. As well as medium long shooting. She would happily take a long range shot at Cutter. If the opportunity presented itself. But Tim's explosives may save her the trouble. Cutter might just blow himself up. If he would Particle Bore into the right location.

Suddenly, way off to the left, about a mile out in the desert. They both could see something. A light. It was intermittent. Like behind a rock, then in front of it.

"What do you think of that Alli? We've got one sensor going off behind the complex and a light way out in the front forty. Wow! It just went out."

"I don't like it Tim. I'm moving out to the left. I'll flank it and the building. I'll use the trucks for cover as long as I can."

"Ok, but remember, let him get into range. I'm sure he's got lots of tricks up his pants."

"Ya? Well wait till he comes across one of your pole inventions. That will blow his pants off." With that Alli moved out.

It was still dark enough to allow Alli cover. Stealth was important, but at this point who knew what they were dealing with. Cutters' unpredictability was the war. If he came for them straight on, he would eventually show himself. The odds were against that scenario. Their profile said he was the type to hang back. They had to rely on good old fashion eye sight as well as the numerous sensors and cameras.

Alli stayed low. A weapon in both hands. She had to reach a position that allowed her to see the open desert, the compound, and the blind. Hugging the trucks, she moved out to the left where the road gently curved back to the desert. She moved from one vehicle to the next. Stopping to listen with every move. The desert was silent. The kind of silence that precedes every morning before the birds and other wildlife start in. Alli thought it felt unusual. It seemed darker.

None of the explosives had gone off. The sensor alert may have been false. That did not explain the light in the desert.

Tim trusted nothing. He stayed glued to the sensor board. Watching for anything that would help pin down the enemies location. Suddenly, Allis' soft voice came over Tim's headset.

"Keep that damn protection device with you, Tim. Don't you loose it! Please!" He responded with his own question.

"How far out are you?" He wanted to know exactly where she was. "And it better not be too far!"

"Fifty yards. Max!"

"Your back to the road?"

"Yes."

"What the hell?" Tim saw something coming off the desert on to the road. It was on Allis' side. Two hundred yards farther out.

"I see it Tim." She spoke up before Tim could alert her.

"Three floaters, Tim. Three!" Alli spoke as quietly as she could. But her heart pounded. She would never get over seeing people floating. She began to feel vulnerable. Exposed. There were two women and a man floating toward them on the road.

"Copy, Alli. Three." Tim's first instinct was to run to her side. They had played this scenario over, and over. They had to stick to the plan. Tim had to stay at his post. No second quessing. No improvising.

The world war had begun. The first shot rang out as the sun tipped over the mountains. Alli killed one of the women, then another. There was no thought to her order. Just expediency in targeting.

There was an explosion out back of the corn. A blood curdling scream came from the individual that took the brunt of the blast. He probably woke up at the very instant of death.

They were Cutter's pawns. Controlled individuals Sent toward the DOA site from different directions. It was logical that Cutter would take this route. Use susceptible people to draw fire and disclose position. That would be the price. Dead innocents.

Sensors went off at Tim's right. He hit some buttons on his console. The result was massive. He could hear many screaming people. The pawns screamed the moment they were hit. Most floated about four to eight feet above the ground. When they were hit by the explosives, they were torn apart. Awful death. Still there was no sign of Cutter. His cowardice still in place. There was no telling how many innocent people he would kill to accomplish his goal. They were nothing more than pawns.

Alli was feeling exposed. With her first salvo she may have alerted Cutter to her position. She headed back to the blind. She alerted Tim that she was returning, but at that moment a man floated out between two trucks. This time it was the shot gun. Before he went down he looked at her with such surprise. She almost threw up.

"Did you feel anything? Did you feel anything?" She repeated. Her voice increasing in volume. She had to dismiss what had happened. There was no time. But haunt her for the rest of her life.

She reached the blind and peered in.

"Tim, are you all right?" He grabbed her and held on. He saw what had taken place. He saw her rip a man apart with her shotgun. It was etched in his mind. The scene was painful. He watched it all on the monitors.

"I'm all right, Alli. I'm sorry you had to go through that. You're doing all the real work."

"I was a little frightened. I needed to come back. Just for a moment." She was feeling sick. Killing innocent people was not the objective.

"I take it you haven't seen Cutter."

"No. I've been watching every monitor. He's not close by."

"This is horrible. These poor people." Alli's heart was breaking. But she knew it was going to be bad.

"Can you still do your job?" Tim asked.

"I'll do my job. If somebody up there helps me."

This was a horrible thing. But it had been decided. If the pawns reached the detectives, all could be lost. If they were killed, the surface might not survive.

Governments could collapse. The military might not be enough to stop Cutter. In his insanity, mass murder could be the first step in his desire for global reign. War would not last long. Many would give up. Surrender their lives to whatever.

What if the Granitarians had to show themselves. With the detectives gone, the surface would be in chaos. The Granitarians might feel they have no other choice. The knowledge of their existence could help tear the world apart. Their peaceful ways, not understood. Even if the Granitarians could stop Cutter, the damage would be done. People might loose their minds. Once it was known that a second society lived beneath them. All this time.

Any scenario that ended with Alli and Tim not surviving, was not welcome. They were not expendable. Many pawns would have to die. This was the one and only chance to right a terrible wrong.

Chapter 37

Emotions aside, the detectives had achieved the upper hand. Their plan worked. They succeeded in luring Cutter to Nevada. In reality, it was a miracle he fell for it at all. They tricked him. Now they had to find him. He was there. Just not in plain sight.

Alli made it her duty to bring up questions that were not previously discussed. Like,

"How many pawns did he send? They just keep coming." Tim only took his eyes off the monitors long enough to give her a look of confusion.

"How did they get here, Tim?" Again, no answer. She calculated that Cutter was getting a little smarter. A little quicker. Using his toy. He'd had a lot of time to play with stolen technology. A lot of time to plan. Manipulating innocents. That was an art. His attack was relentless.

There were more explosions in the wheat fields. Watching the monitors, they could see the pawns floating. Just above the wheat. It was an eerie sight. Smoke from the explosions added to the effect. Like a scary fog rolling in. Pawns passed through it. Disappearing for a moment, then reappearing. Sometimes with arms outstretched. No thought, just touch anyone.

Alli was preparing to go back out, when Tim grabbed her arm.

"What if we do get him? If we kill Cutter, would the pawns wake up? They might not know where they were, but they'd be alive."

"I don't know, Partner! I just want to shoot him. These people don't deserve this. They don't deserve to die for him!"

"I know! But nothing has gone off inside. He's got to believe we're in there." Tim caught a glimpse of something out in the desert.

"Oh, my God! Look!" From behind and to the left of the blind were two rows of six floaters. They had skirted around the fields and were now coming down the road. Tim could see them on the monitors.

"Wow!" He said. He turned all the lights on. The entire area was lit up. One row would probably run into his traps. They were planted high enough to take out floaters. Some would miss them. One or two pawns, anyway. Alli reloaded both her chosen weapons.

"I feel like an idiot at a carnival shooting steel ducks! It makes me sick!" Yet she leaned down and found the gun hole in the blind. If any pawns got through, she would do her job.

"Tim, I'm going to aim at men first. We're looking for a man. Unless absolutely necessary I'm going to avoid women. If I hit him, we're going to know it!"

Every action made by the pawns was orchestrated. The direction they came, how fast or how slow. All to accomplish two objectives. To root out the detectives. Or others in military seniority. Two. To shield himself from any contact until he felt comfortable. He was there. Watching from a hilltop. Enjoying the show. Through a pair of binoculars. But he only saw his pawns go down. He never saw the shooters. He scanned the high ground that flanked the DOA site. Looking for high velocity rounds shot from a distance. There were none.

"What's going on down there? What does this task force got going?" Cutter had taken on a fake southern accent since leaving Miami.

"Their personal are well hidden. We'll just have to root em out."

His plan was in motion. Keep wave after wave of innocent pawns hitting the compound. Take out as many soldiers, and government agents as possible before he had to make his move. Curious though, why hadn't he seen a larger military presence? There were lots of vehicles, but no soldiers.

Cutter decided it was time for a little search and destroy. He used Particle Boring to send three pawns into the building. The next few seconds were horrifying. Tim watched it on the monitors. As soon as they hit the trip wires, the blast cut them to pieces. The cameras were destroyed as well. Turning Tim's monitors to black.

The pawns attacked and went down. Some looking as if they'd physically changed. Their faces contorting when not reaching their objectives. Almost as if they were being punished. Through the scope of her 308 rifle, Alli got a clear view of her targets. She had a hard task. She didn't hesitate.

Chapter 38

Cutter's delusional state reached a fever pitch. From his perch on the hillside, his coveted device directed his pawns on their mission of death. But most were sacrificed. He was sure to discover were the high ranking officials were hiding. His hated detectives were too low on the totem for an operation like this. Capturing him, was a career maker.

They were probably politicians he'd have to deal with anyway. Ones that would oppose him when he came to power. Better to get rid of them now.

Soldiers could be in the trucks. Or entrenched. In fox holes. But the building held the most interest. Higher ups must be housed there.

Sending the pawns in at different angles of attack, some hovered in and around the vehicles. Trying to root them out. Pawns attacking from the far side of the building were met with explosions, but still he saw no soldiers.

Cutter was amazingly accurate using Granitarian technology. He sent two groups of pawns toward the building. As they got closer, more explosions. It reinforced Cutter's belief that his foes were protecting the building, because of who was in it.

Back when Tim Renolds was schooling Alli on military tactics, he touched on this particular scenario. Protect a useless structure, or point on a map. Convince your enemy of its importance. That was the bait, Bring him in close. The closer he got, the more resistance. When the pawns were near the door, incendiaries lit up the sky. The explosion hot enough, they felt it in the blind.

But of course, the building was empty. The pawns that got in before, were dead. Cutter may have thought they were still doing his work. But they were dead.

But he was running out of time. He had another task to complete. It was time to find out if the Space Station could stay in orbit after sustaining a powerful internal blast. He doubt it could. It was rigged and ready to go. All he needed was a moment to set it off. However, he suspected it had become a Granitarian trap. He understood their cunning. They could be near by. They scared him.

Particle Boring off the hill, he left his pawns to do battle. He instantly appeared in the center section. Inches away from the bomb. Though zero gravity slowed him down, it only took a second to hit an electronic fuse. That gave him five seconds to escape.

At that very moment, a Granitarian saucer detected his presence and opened fire. Between their weapon and the bomb inside, the Space Station disintegrated. The blast was visible from the surface. Hundreds of pieces fell back to Earth. A sad tribute to its crew.

The surface was presented a beautiful light show. Most thought it was a meteor. Not the remains of one of man kinds greatest achievements. No historical record would be kept. How the Space Station died would be known to two people. All part of their greater secret. Behind closed doors, some would mention strange circumstances surrounding the disappearance of the crew. Prior to the explosion that ultimately destroyed it. But the Space agency felt it best to report a catastrophic failure and leave it at that.

Ceremonies were held for the crew, and family members. High ranking military and political types were urged to attend. The media was not allowed. But soon after, many politicians gave speeches. The media did attend those. The men and women speaking had no idea what they were talking about. But none waisted the opportunity. Politics has always been about timing. If there is a stage, climb high. Smile for the cameras.

Parked on a highway. Less than one mile from the DOA site. Were six long semi-truck trailers. Three men, two Russians and an American, delivered them. They made two runs each. Using stolen dollars, Cutter had them fitted to transport his pawns. He hired the drivers after first checking to see if they were susceptible to the effects of his device. They were not. Secondly, and more important to Cutter, was the fact they were ex-cons. Willing to do anything for large amounts of money. There was a shock factor when they first saw what they were transporting, but the hundred-thousand dollars each would receive, softened the blow. Their only job was to drive the trailers to a certain location and open the rear doors. One at a time. Every thirty minutes. When the cargo was gone, they were free to leave. Each trailer carried fifty pawns.

Chapter 39

Back at the DOA site, the war raged on. Alli had no way of knowing how many people were affected. How many have been sacrificed. As she stared out across the desert, she could see women. They kept coming in groups of three and six. Alli hated the slaughter. But if they got too close....

It was about Tim. Protecting him was her responsibility. The blind, the compound. Her responsibility. Pawns floated off the road. Directly toward her. The desert had no natural barrier. Now the attack came from all sides.

Instinctively, both detectives moved out. Before he left the blind, Tim set off the remaining explosives. The blasts were all around them. Some pawns were hit. But most got through.

Alli went right, Tim left. Alli firing her .308 cal from the eye. Hitting everything she aimed at. Tim pulled his .45 caliber. He ran straight at the pawns. Emptying one clip, loading another. One pawn came up behind him. Alli shot it dead from 25 yards away. Tim glanced at her. He grinned. Raising an eyebrow. She was his kind of girl.

The problem was, they were in the open. Exposed. They had to figure Cutter could see them. He could. He had returned to his vantage point. Barely avoiding the Granitarians at the Space Station. As soon as he looked down at the DOA site, he saw them. He picked up his binoculars. The war was right where he had left it. As he did, he was stuck by a massive beam of energy. There before him, hovering just off the hill, was the second ship. It had never left. It was there all along. Watching over the detectives. The large triangular craft, trapped Martin Cutter. He hit buttons on the device. Trying to escape. But the beam held him fast. His device no longer worked.

The occupants of the spacecraft, brought Cutter aboard. He was immediately put into a chamber. Where he was unable to move. Unable to speak. His fate had been decided. But it was complicated.

Alli's guide faced Cutter through a window in the chamber. Though it was widely held, that if Cutter was ever taken alive, he would be put to death. It was the only fitting punishment.

"You have done much damage, Martin Cutter. What do we do with you now?" Cutter could not answer. But if he could, he would have screamed. Over the Granitarians shoulder, in the shadows of the ship, Cutter could see a small, grey, figure marching toward his prison. As it got closer, it raised a limb. As if pushing away evil.

Chapter 40

The moment Cutter lost control over the drowns, they fell to the ground. Bruised, but alive.

The detectives continued defending the DOA site. Unaware their enemy was now the guest of an alien race.

Alli searched for targets. But they had dropped out of sight. Behind sage brush, rocks, wheat, and corn. Tim saw what was happening, and ran to Alli's side.

Alli searched for targets.

"Back off, Alli. Back, Off!" Tim rested his hand on her shoulder. She stopped firing, and eased up. Her rifle pulled to a resting position.

"Look out there." Tim pointed to the closest pawns lying dazed on the ground.

"Did you hit Cutter?" He asked.

"I don't know. I don't think so." Alli was a bit confused. "Where is he? Did you blow him up, Tim? We have to see the body."

Running past the trucks, onto the desert, they were confronted by a hovering space craft. Four Granitarians stood below the craft. In their custody was Martin Cutter. The insane killer. The animal that tried to change history. Alli's guide lead the way.

"They've got him!" She Screamed. "They've got Cutter!" She raised her weapon over her head. Waving it in defiance. Running to meet the ship, they found Cutter restrained. Removed from his prison. Displayed for the detectives.

"Allison, you have done well. His crimes are massive... Terrible and thought less. They deserve unique attention. But I'm not sure we are the ones to make that decision." Alli's guide deeply respected her. But there was more. He reached out to touch her. But pulled back. Afraid he'd be telling her too much.

Cutter was restrained. Alli moved toward him with purpose. When she was face to face, she gently head butted him. Any harder, she would have knocked him out. She stunned him. He had no where to run.

"Do you know who I am? I'm the one who has been chasing you. The Granitarians are sweet people. But I'm not. They never discipline their own. They don't have to."

In Granitarian society, there is no capitol punishment. There was no need. The last and only time a Granitarian broke the rules, he was removed from Earth. That was a very long time ago.

Chapter 41

The chamber that had held Martin Cutter, was not made to be a prison. IT was designed for medical procedures. However, any procedure on Cutter, would have killed him. His prison was not made for humans. The spacecraft belonged to the aliens. Alli's guide was just along for the ride.

Cutter's fate was complicated. He should be destroyed. He should be turned over to the aliens. Left in their hands, a suitable, all be it, horrible form of execution would take place. They had no problem with it. Their feelings about humans were somewhat mixed. Especially regarding the billions on the surface.

But Granitarians were compassionate. Destroying Cutter was not necessarily the answer. He was not of their society.

Alli recognized a Granitarian woman that stood near by. She spoke at their open air complex.

"Allison Chapman. You will always be welcome. Your partner as well. You're really quite extraordinary. We will keep a place for you. We need to learn more about each other. When you return home, you will find a gift. We are truly sorry for what Cutter has done. The Aliens will take him if you wish. It is our ultimate punishment."

Cutter was gagged, but screamed in terror at the prospect of being turned over to the aliens. Tim looked at Alli, then to the Granitarians.

"Could you give us a moment?" He took Alli aside and whispered in her ear.

"I'd love to turn him over. I'd like to see what they'd do. But he's ours. He's subject to our laws."

Alli started to speak, then stopped. She shook her head in agreement.

Tim moved toward Cutter and grabbed him by the restraints.

"Don't think you're getting off easy. Sorry I missed you in Peru." Tim pulled his gun, pressing it hard against Cutter's head.

"He'll be put away." He said. "Where he's going, there's no escape."

As soon as the transfer was complete, the female Granitarian whispered something to Alli's guide. Whatever she said agitated him. It was obvious he was unhappy with her. Their voices grew louder.

"Your not going to tell her? The woman asked. "She has the right to know." This brought on a stern look from the guide.

"No. It's not time." Alli overheard the conversation. The woman ran to Alli and embraced her.

"There are aspects of your life, that not only effect you, but effect us as well. You are very important, Allison. We don't have time to talk now, but soon. We will contact you. Remember, always carry your protection devices. We must go now."

The Granitarians disappeared. Each leaving a small pin hole of light. The ship rose, then sped away. Alli watched until it became a dot in the sky. Then it was gone. It only took a moment.

Behind her, Cutter began crying.

"Shut up!" Tim yanked back on the bands around Cutter's wrists. He wanted to shoot him. But his trial had already taken place. Cutter's fate was decided. He would never tell anybody, anything, ever again. He was being delivered just a few miles away. To the most secret jail in the world. Area 51! Rules there are simple. You go in. You don't come out. No one talks to you. Ever. Totally cut off. It seems there are good reasons for prisons like that.

Alli ran to the remaining pawns. Who were now survivors. They would be helped. But a story had to be perpetrated to keep the secret. They were told 'The Phenomenon Killer" drugged and kidnaped them. The survivors, as well as the rest of world, believed the story. It seemed logical.

By the time the sun had fully risen, it was over. Special military units came in to clean up. Dressed in white clean suits, the DOA site was returned to it's natural condition. Left just as the detectives found it. It was as if the event never happened.

Agent Chapman and detective Renolds would remain unnoticed. There were questions, but "The Phenomenon" was dead. Or so the press was told. "The Phenomenon" technology was unfortunately destroyed during the apprehension of the mass murderer. No trace could be found. The killing stopped. That was what mattered. The military took credit for the capture. It was only fair. Their trucks were used. That was a major contribution. As for UFO reports. They were passed on to a "Special Department" of the FBI. Never to be heard from again.

The effect on the world would not be what Cutter envisioned.

Destroying the space station would not be the catalyst for war. Martin Cutter was wrong. For a time, countries began asking for stronger alliances. The strange murders overwhelmed the politicians. Some tried to lie. Some politicized. No one believed the politicians. For the most part, their days were numbered. It was time for new blood. The word was out about a strange and powerful device the killer used. Miami saw to that. No one knew where it came from, but incredible stories would be told for years.

Unfortunately, Cutters era would become legend. People blamed him for hundreds of deaths. His name would be linked with Hitler and Stalin. It seems, mass murders always receive a place in history.

The United States would remain strong. It's people are what make it powerful. Following the capture of Martin Cutter, the economy grew. There was a calming affect on the world as a whole. People felt safe again.

However, after a few months, the press started noticing small changes in government. It started with the President dismissing certain cabinet members. Appointees he had made, but no longer needed. The positions then, were not filed. A very slow dismissal of key individuals within special departments. It was what could only be called a cleansing. A sanitizing of government employees. A secret society was taking over. But it would be years before the extent of the plan was known. It was an infection that allowed power hungry individuals to move freely throughout our core. This infection would reach other countries as well. A change had begun.

"Allison! We don't have much time." Her guide stepped forward and gently squeezed her hand. Then pulled her close, giving her a hug. When he looked in her eyes, she thought of her father.

"After some thought, we believe we must turn Cutter over to you. He is your prisoner. He is from your world. We are responsible for what he has done, and are truly sorry for that. Our futures depended on his capture. We needed your help. We owe you our thanks." For a few moments Alli stared at him. It had been a long day. Her guide turned from side to side, surveying the land scape.

"It's beautiful on the surface, Allison. We know what we are missing. But the billions of people above, are not prepared for us."

"We have another option to discuss. If you wish, the aliens are happy to dispose of him. But that is a decision you must make. We can't make it for you."

Alli stepped back. When she reached Tim, she took his arm. What her guide was suggesting.

"This is an alien ship?" She asked.

"These guys are aliens?" Tim repeated.

"Yes detective. They were here all the time. Keeping an eye on you. Keeping you safe. Making sure we would never loose you."

Alli wished the Granitarians had mention the aliens sooner.

"I saw that ship. It was in your airport the first time I went to Granitaria."

"That is correct." He responded.

"You didn't tell me they were there."

"Allison, there are a lot of things we haven't told you. Give it time. Now, you must make a decision."

Alli was surprised. But she knew there was little time for banter. Tim leaned over and whispered,

"Aliens? That's something you don't hear every day." Alli ignored him. This was no time for levity.

Chapter 42

When Alli returned home, she found a small perfectly wrapped box in the middle of her living room floor. It had a beautifully cut square piece of moss on top. It was obvious where it came from. When unwrapped, she found the box was made of quartz crystal cut so precise she could see through it. She raised the top and found it full of rare, valuable gems. Maybe from Peru? No matter. There were agency rules. She could bury them. Alli began to cry. She was very tired.

As for Tim, he sat quietly at a near by burger joint. The place was full. Conversations from the other tables were amplified by ugly, sterile, tile placed there when a large corporation bought out the mom and pop. He remembered it having a bright, clean atmosphere. Back when he entertained cops, or informants. It was his preferred meeting place. An off sight place to do interviews. A place to unwind. Talk to the man on the street. Families. Every day people. It still had descent food. But now he felt uneasy. Apprehensive. What if he were to blurt out secrets? There were so many. Who besides Alli could he trust?

They were locked together for all time. Their secrets were real secrets.

At the end of that day. Before Tim and Alli left the DOA site, Tim asked the wrong question.

"Excuse me, What's the purpose of this place? We were never told."

Like sounding the dinner bell, the soldiers stopped working. A thin young doctor type appeared out of no where. His demeanor was arrogant. He demanded any paper work Tim could provide. Knowing damn well who Tim Renolds was.

Tim offered up his Phoenix identification. The "doctor Type" ripped it from his hand. Tim thought this guy was trying to assert himself into the conversation. His demeanor was arrogant. He demanded any paperwork Tim could provide. Knowing damn well who Tim was, and what he had accomplished.

He demanded any paper work Tim could provide. Knowing damn well who Tim Renolds was, and what he had just accomplished? Tim offered up his Phoenix police identification. The "Doctor Type," ripped it from his hand. Tim's estimation was the guy was trying to get a promotion. Insert himself. Tim restrained. He could care less what this persons "progressive" tendencies were.

"Detective Renolds, we're not here to indulge you. Don't ever talk about this place again. You shouldn't be here." Tim made no further attempt to carry on the conversation. The scene was strange. Like he showed up to a party and no one knew him. Every single military person on site stared at him. Their message was clear. We know something that you don't. Don't mess with us.

Though Alli missed the confrontation, Tim alerted her later. With all they'd been through. Saving people's lives. Making the world safer. The military's reaction seemed a little harsh. Something was being protected. Or covered up. Either or, someone did not like their using the Nevada DOA site. Person or persons unknown were nervous.

For Tim and Alli the DOA site was a second home. They knew inside and out. It would forever be a part of their lives. They would return. The lower floors pointed the way to White Candle. Affirming the Granitarian story. But there was the nagging question.

"What was White Candle?" Not even the Granitarians could say.

It took Tim a long time to eat his meal. Like his companion, he wanted to remember everything. The Granitarians. The ship they went aboard. Alli's stories. Two hours went by before he left the hamburger joint.

Two days later, still recovering from the battle, Alli invited Tim to lunch at her home. When he arrived they stood in the doorway holding each other. Alli held on for what seemed like a long time. What transpired at the DOA site took it's toll. Alli had to pull the trigger. She killed a lot of people. They both did.

Later, the discussion turned to Granitaria. How their day to day lives had changed. Each of their abilities to evaluate the world around them, had changed. Both detectives felt everything was different. From people to space travel. Oceans, to walking down the street. It was all different. They would never look at their world the same way.

They discussed the murders and how many families must have been affected.

They also made a promise to one another. To return to Peru, and maybe some other locations.

Finally, Alli and Tim tried to make sense of White Candle. The Granitarians warned them it was dangerous. Almost as if it scared them. What was it? Government? Or more behind the scenes. Deep state? Between the DOA site, and the warning from her guide, White Candle had to be shadow government. To effect the Granitarians, the way they described, something on the surface must have made a lot of noise. Noise they could detect.

However, Alli pointed out, that her guide held back from telling all that they knew about White Candle. She could tell.

Tim wanted to go back to the DOA site.

"When everything settles down, I'd like to go. Just to see if anything has changed. I want to see if anything was removed from the labs." Alli agreed. That had crossed her mind as well. The site would always hold a special compelling, attraction. Throughout their lives, they would visit it many times.

No matter what White Candle might be, the two warriors knew something was coming. However, now they could rest. Though the credit for capturing Cutter would be withheld, their respective employers knew damn well what they had done. To that point. They were awarded 30 days vacation.

Alli asked Tim to close his eyes. She had a surprise for him. He did what she asked.

"Now open." She said. Tim stared down at the chest full of gem stones. His immediate reaction was to conjure up his nervous word. His way of dealing with any surprise. The sound of a "W" may have left his lips. But in that split second he stopped himself from finishing the word. Like quitting a vice. He promised never to say it again. It was time for old habits to be removed. Replaced by love, truth, and caution. Tim Renolds was in love. He would spend the rest of his life protecting Alli Chapman. Their adventure was just beginning.

Printed in the United States
By Bookmasters